THE TRUTH BEHIND
HIS TOUCH

THE TRUTH BEHIND HIS TOUCH

BY

CATHY WILLIAMS

First published in Great Britain 2012
by Mills & Boon, an imprint of Harlequin (UK) Limited.
Large Print edition 2012
Harlequin (UK) Limited, Eton House,
18-24 Paradise Road, Richmond, Surrey TW9 1SR

© Cathy Williams 2012

ISBN: 978 0 263 22617 1

Harlequin (UK) policy is to use papers that are natural,
renewable and recyclable products and made from
wood grown in sustainable forests. The logging and
manufacturing process conform to the legal environmental
regulations of the country of origin.

Printed and bound in Great Britain
by CPI Antony Rowe, Chippenham, Wiltshire

CHAPTER ONE

CAROLINE fanned herself wearily with the guide book which she had been clutching like a talisman ever since she had disembarked from the plane at Malpensa airport in Milan, and took the time to look around her. Somewhere, nestled amongst these ancient, historic buildings and wide, elegant *piazzas*, lay her quarry. She knew that she should be heading directly there, bypassing all temptations of a cold drink and something sweet, sticky, chocolatey and deliciously fattening, but she was hot, she was exhausted and she was ravenous.

'It will take you no time at all!' Alberto had said encouragingly. 'One short flight, Caroline. And a taxi… Maybe a little walking to find his offices, but what sights you'll see. The Duomo. You will never have laid eyes on anything so spectacular. *Palazzos.* More than you can shake a stick at. And the shops. Well, it is many, many years since I have been to Milan, but I can still recall the splendour of the Vittorio Gallery.'

Caroline had looked at him with raised, sceptical eyebrows and the old man had had the grace to flush sheepishly, because this trip to Milan was hardly a sightseeing tour. In fact, she was expected back within forty-eight hours and her heart clenched anxiously at the expectations sitting heavily on her shoulders.

She was to locate Giancarlo de Vito, run him to ground and somehow return to Lake Como with him.

'I would go myself, my dear,' Alberto had murmured, 'but my health does not permit it. The doctor said that I have to rest as much as possible—the strain on my heart… I am not a well man, you understand…'

Caroline wondered, not for the first time, how she had managed to let herself get talked into this mission but there seemed little point dwelling on that. She was here now, surrounded by a million people, perspiring in soaring July temperatures, and it was just too late in the day to have a sudden attack of nerves.

The truth was that the success or failure of this

trip was really not her concern. She was the messenger. Alberto, yes, *he* would be affected, but she was really just his personal assistant who happened to be performing a slightly bizarre duty.

Someone bumped into her from behind and she hastily consulted her map and began walking towards the small street which she had highlighted in bold orange.

She had dressed inappropriately for the trip, but it had been cooler by the lake. Here, it was sweltering and her cream trousers stuck to her legs like glue. The plain yellow blouse with its three-quarter-length sleeves had looked suitably smart when she had commenced her journey but now she wished that she had worn something without sleeves, and she should have done something clever with her hair. Put it up into some kind of bun, perhaps. Yes; she had managed to twist it into a long braid of sorts but it kept unravelling and somehow getting itself plastered around her neck.

Caught up in her own physical discomfort and the awkwardness of what lay ahead, she barely noticed the old mellow beauty of the cathedral with its impressive buttresses, spires and statues as she hurried past it, dragging her suitcase which behaved like a recalcitrant child, stopping and swerving and doing its best to misbehave.

Anyone with a less cheerful and equable temperament might have been tempted to curse the elderly employer who had sent them on this impossible mission, which was frankly way beyond the scope of their duties. But Caroline, tired, hot and hungry as she was, was optimistic that she could do what was expected of her. She had enormous faith in human nature. Alberto, on the other hand, was the world's most confirmed pessimist.

She very nearly missed the building. Not knowing what exactly to expect, she had imagined something along the lines of an office in London. Bland, uninspiring, with perhaps too much glass and too little imagination.

Retracing her steps, she looked down at the address which she had carefully printed on an index card, and then up at the ancient exterior of stone and soft, aged pinks, no more than three storeys tall, adorned with exquisite carvings and fronted by two stone columns.

How difficult could Giancarlo be if he worked

in this wonderful place? Caroline mused, heart lightening.

'I cannot tell you anything of Giancarlo,' Alberto had said mournfully when she had tried to press him for details of what she would be letting herself in for. 'It is many, many years since I have seen him. I could show you some pictures, but they are so out of date. He would have changed in all these years… If I had a computer… But an old man like me… How could I ever learn now to work one of those things?'

'I could go and get my laptop from upstairs,' she had offered instantly, but he had waved her down.

'No, no. I don't care for those gadgets. Televisions and telephones are as far as I am prepared to go when it comes to technology.'

Privately, Caroline agreed with him. She used her computer to email but that was all, and it was nigh on impossible trying to access the Internet in the house anyway.

So she had few details on which to go. She suspected, however, that Giancarlo was rich, because Alberto had told her in passing that he had 'made something of himself'. Her suspicion crystallised when she stepped into the cool, ubermodern, marbled portico of Giancarlo's offices. If the façade of the building looked as though it had stepped out of an architectural guide to mediaeval buildings, inside the twenty-first century had made its mark.

Only the cool, pale marble underfoot and the scattering of old masterpieces on the walls hinted at the age of the building.

Of course, she wasn't expected. Surprise, apparently, was of the utmost importance, 'or else he will just refuse to see you, I am convinced of it!'.

It took her over thirty-five minutes to try to persuade the elegant receptionist positioned like a guard dog behind her wood-and-marble counter, who spoke far too quickly for Caroline to follow, that she shouldn't be chucked out.

'What is your business here?'

'Ah…'

'Are you expected?'

'Not *exactly*…'

'Are you aware that Signore de Vito is an extremely important man?'

'Er…' Then she had practised her haltering Italian and explained the connection to Giancarlo, produced several documents which had been pored over in silence and the wheels of machinery had finally begun to move.

But still she would have to wait.

Three floors up, Giancarlo, in the middle of a meeting with three corporate financiers, was interrupted by his secretary, who whispered something in his ear that made him still and brought the shutters down on his dark, cold eyes.

'Are you sure?' he asked in a clipped voice. Elena Carli seldom made mistakes; it was why she had worked for him so successfully for the past five-and-a-half years. She did her job with breathtaking efficiency, obeyed orders without question and *seldom* made mistakes. When she nodded firmly, he immediately got to his feet, made his excuses—though not profusely, because these financiers needed him far more than he needed them—and then, meeting dismissed, he walked across to the window to stare down at the paved, private courtyard onto which his offices backed.

So the past he thought to have left behind was returning. Good sense counselled him to turn his back on this unexpected intrusion in his life, but he was curious and what harm would there be in indulging his curiosity? In his life of unimaginable wealth and vast power, curiosity was a rare visitor, after all.

Giancarlo de Vito had been ferociously single-minded and ruthlessly ambitious to get where he was now. He had had no choice. His mother had needed to be kept and after a series of unfortunate lovers the only person left to keep her had been him. He had finished his university career with a first and had launched himself into the world of high finance with such dazzling expertise that it hadn't been long before doors began to open. Within three years of finishing university, he'd been able to pick and choose his employer. Within five years, he'd no longer needed an employer because he had become the powerhouse who did the employing. Now, at just over thirty, he had become a billionaire, diversifying with gratifying success, branching out and stealing the march on competitors with every successive merger and acquisition and in the process building himself a reputation that rendered him virtually untouchable.

His mother had seen only the tip of his enormous success, as she had died six years previously—perhaps, fittingly, in the passenger seat

of her young lover's fast car—a victim, as he
had seen it, of a life gone wrong. As her only
offspring, Giancarlo knew he should have been
more heartbroken than he actually was, but his
mother had been a temperamental and difficult
woman, fond of spending money and easily dis-
satisfied. He had found her flitting from lover
to lover rather distasteful, but never had he once
criticized her. At the end of the day, hadn't she
been through enough?

Unaccustomed to taking these trips down memory lane, Giancarlo shook himself out of his in-
trospection with a certain amount of impatience.
Presumably the woman who had come to see him
and who was currently sitting in the grand marble
foyer was to blame for his lapse in self-control.
With his thoughts back in order and back where
they belonged, he buzzed her up.

'You may go up now.' The receptionist beck-
oned to Caroline, who could have stayed sitting
in the air-conditioned foyer quite happily for another few hours. Her feet were killing her and she
had finally begun cooling down after the hours
spent in the suffocating heat. 'Signora Carli will
meet you up at the top of the elevator and show

you to Signore De Vito's office. If you like, you may leave your…case here.'

Caroline thought that the last thing the receptionist seemed to want was her battered pull-along being left anywhere in the foyer. At any rate, she needed it with her.

And, now that she was finally here, she felt a little twist of nervousness at the prospect of what lay ahead. She wouldn't want to return to the lake house empty-handed. Alberto had suffered a heart attack several weeks previously. His health was not good and, his doctor had confided in her, the less stress the better.

With a determined lift of her head, Caroline followed the personal assistant in silence, passing offices which seemed abnormally silent, staffed with lots of hard-working executives who barely looked up as they walked past.

Everyone seemed very well-groomed. The women were all thin, good-looking and severe, with their hair scraped back and their suits shrieking of money well spent.

In comparison, Caroline felt overweight, short and dishevelled. She had never been skinny, even as a child. When she sucked her breath in and looked at herself sideways through narrowed eyes, she could almost convince herself that she was curvy and voluptuous, but the illusion was always destroyed the second she took a harder look at her reflection. Nor was her hair of the manageable variety. It rarely did as it was told; it flowed in wild abandon down her back and was only ever remotely obedient when it was wet. Right now the heat had added more curl than normal and she knew that tendrils were flying wildly out of their impromptu braid. She had to keep blowing them off her face.

After trailing along behind Elena—who had introduced herself briefly and then seen fit to say absolutely nothing else on the way up—a door was opened into an office so exquisite that for a few seconds Caroline wasn't even aware that she had been deposited like an unwanted parcel, nor did she notice the man by the window turning slowly around to look at her.

All she could see was the expanse of splendid, antique Persian rug on the marble floor; the soft, silk wallpaper on the walls; the smooth, dark patina of a bookshelf that half-filled an entire wall; the warm, old paintings on the walls—not paintings of silly lines and shapes that no one could ever decipher, but paintings of beautiful land-scapes, heavy with trees and rivers.

'Wow,' she breathed, deeply impressed as she continued to look around her with shameless awe.

At long last her eyes rested on the man staring at her and she was overcome with a suffocating, giddy sensation as she absorbed the wild, impossible beauty of his face. Black hair, combed back and ever so slightly too long, framed a face of stunning perfection. His features were classically perfect and invested with a raw sensuality that brought a heated flush to her cheeks. His eyes were dark and unreadable. Expensive, lovingly hand-tailored charcoal-grey trousers sheathed long legs and the crisp white shirt rolled to the elbows revealed strong, bronzed forearms with a sprinkling of dark hair. In the space of a few seconds, Caroline realised that she was staring at the most spectacular-looking man she had ever clapped eyes on in her life. She also belatedly realised that she was gaping, mouth inelegantly open, and she cleared her throat in an attempt to get a hold of herself.

The silence stretched to breaking point and then

at last the man spoke and introduced himself, inviting her to take a seat, which she was only too happy to do because her legs felt like jelly. His voice matched his appearance. It was deep, dark, smooth and velvety. It was also icy cold, and a trickle of doubt began creeping in, because this was not a man who looked as though he could be persuaded into doing anything he didn't want to do.

'So...' Giancarlo sat down, pushing himself away from his desk so that he could cross his long legs, and stared at her. 'What makes you think that you can just barge into my offices, Miss...?'

'Rossi. Caroline.'

'I was in the middle of a meeting.'

'I'm so sorry.' She stumbled over the apology. 'I didn't mean to interrupt anything. I would have been happy to wait until you were finished...' Her naturally sunny personality rose to the surface and she offered him a small smile. 'In fact, it was so wonderfully cool in your foyer and I was just so grateful to rest my legs. I've been on the go for absolutely ages and it's as hot as a furnace out there...' In receipt of his continuing and unwelcoming silence, her voice faded away and she licked her lips nervously.

Giancarlo was quite happy to let her stew in her own discomfiture.

'This is a fantastic building, by the way.'

'Let's do away with the pleasantries, Miss Rossi. What are you doing here?'

'Your father sent me.'

'So I gather. Which is why you're sitting in my office. My question is *why*? I haven't had any contact with my father in over fifteen years, so I'm curious as to why he should suddenly decide to send a henchman to get in touch with me.'

Caroline felt an uncustomary warming anger flood through her as she tried to marry up this cold, dark stranger with the old man of whom she was so deeply fond, but getting angry wasn't going to get her anywhere.

'And who *are* you anyway? My father is hardly a spring chicken. Don't tell me that he's managed to find himself a young wife to nurse him faithfully through his old age?' He leaned back in his chair and steepled his fingers together. 'Nothing too beautiful, of course,' he murmured, casting insolent, assessing eyes over her. 'Devotion in the form of a young, beautiful, nubile wife is never a good idea for an old man, even a rich old man...'

'How dare you?'

Giancarlo laughed coldly. 'You show up here, unannounced, with a message from a father who was written out of my life a long time ago... Frankly, I have every right to dare.'

'I am *not* married to your father!'

'Well, now the alternative is even more distasteful, not to mention downright stupid. Why involve yourself with someone three times your age unless you're in it for the financial gain? Don't tell me the sex is breathtaking?'

'I can't believe you're saying these things!' She wondered how she could have been so bowled over by the way he looked when he was obviously a loathsome individual, just the sort of cold, unfeeling, sneering sort she hated. 'I'm not involved with your father in any way other than professionally, *signore*!'

'No? Then what is a young girl like you doing in a rambling old house by a lake with only an old man for company?'

Caroline glared at him. She was still smarting at the way his eyes had roamed over her and dismissed her as 'nothing too beautiful'. She knew she wasn't beautiful but to hear it casually emerge from the mouth of someone she didn't know was beyond rude. Especially from the mouth of someone as physically compelling as the man sitting in front of her. Why hadn't she done what most other people would have in similar circumstances and found herself an Internet café so that she could do some background research on the man she had been told to ferret out? At least then she might have been prepared!

She had to grit her teeth together and fight the irresistible urge to grab her suitcase and jump ship.

'Well? I'm all ears.'

'There's no need to be horrible to me, *signore.* I'm sorry if I've ruined your meeting, or…or whatever you were doing, but I didn't *volunteer* to come here.'

Giancarlo almost didn't believe his ears. People never accused him of being *horrible.* Granted, they might sometimes think that, but it was vaguely shocking to actually *hear* someone come right out and say it. Especially a woman. He was accustomed to women doing everything within their power to please him. He looked narrowly at his uninvited visitor. She was certainly not the sort of rake-thin beauty eulogised in the pages of magazines. She was trying hard to conceal her expression but it was transparently clear that the last place she wanted to be was in his office, being interrogated.

Too bad.

'I take it my father manipulated you into doing what he wanted. Are you his housekeeper? Why would he employ an English housekeeper?'

'I'm his personal assistant,' Caroline admitted reluctantly. 'He used to know my father once upon a time. Your father had a one-year posting in England lecturing at a university and my father was one of his students. He was my father's mentor and they kept in touch after your father returned to Italy. My father is Italian. I think he enjoyed having someone he could speak to in Italian.

'Anyway, I didn't go to university, but my parents thought it would be nice for me to learn Italian, seeing that it's my father's native tongue, and he asked Alberto if he could help me find a posting over here for a few months. So I'm helping your father with his memoirs and also pretty much taking care of all the admin—stuff like that. Don't you want to know…um…how he is? You haven't seen him in such a long time.'

'If I had wanted to see my father, don't you think I would have contacted him before now?'

'Yes, well, pride can sometimes get in the way of us doing what we want to do.'

'If your aim is to play amateur psychologist, then the door is right behind you. Avail yourself of it.'

'I'm not playing amateur psychologist,' Caroline persisted stubbornly. 'I just think, well, I know that it probably wasn't ideal when your parents got divorced. Alberto doesn't talk much about it, but I know that when your mother walked out and took you with her you were only twelve…'

'I don't believe I'm hearing this!' Intensely private, Giancarlo could scarcely credit that he was listening to someone drag his past out of the closet in which it had been very firmly shut.

'How else am I supposed to deal with this situation?' Caroline asked, bewildered and dismayed.

'I am not in the habit of discussing my past!'

'Yes, well, that's not *my* fault.' She felt herself soften. 'Don't you think that it's a good thing to talk about the things that bother us? Don't you *ever* think about your dad?'

His internal line buzzed and he spoke in rapid Italian, telling his secretary to hold all further calls until he advised her otherwise. Suddenly, filled with a restless energy he couldn't seem to contain, he pushed himself away from the desk and moved across to the window to look briefly outside before turning around and staring at the girl on the chair who had swivelled to face him.

She looked as though butter wouldn't melt in her mouth—very young, very innocent and with a face as transparent as a pane of glass. Right now, he seemed to be an object of pity, and he tightened his mouth with a sense of furious outrage.

'He's had a heart attack,' Caroline told him abruptly, her eyes beginning to well up because she was so very fond of him. Having him rushed into hospital, dealing with the horror of it all on her own had been almost more than she could take. 'A very serious one. In fact, for a while it was touch and go.' She opened her satchel, rummaged around for a tissue and found a pristine white handkerchief pressed into her hand.

'Sorry,' she whispered shakily. 'But I don't

know how you can just stand there like a statue and not feel a thing.'

Big brown eyes looked accusingly at him and Giancarlo flushed, annoyed with himself because there was no reason why he should feel guilty on that score. He had no relationship with his father. Indeed, his memories of life in the big house by the lake were a nightmare of parental warfare. Alberto had married his very young and very pretty blonde wife when he had been in his late forties, nearly twenty-five years older than Adriana, and was already a cantankerous and confirmed bachelor.

It had been a marriage that had struggled on against all odds and had been, to all accounts, hellishly difficult for his demanding young wife.

His mother had not held back from telling him everything that had been so horrifically wrong with the relationship, as soon as he had been old enough to appreciate the gory detail. Alberto had been selfish, cold, mean, dismissive, contemptuous and probably, his mother had maintained viciously, would have had other women had he not lacked even basic social skills when it came to the opposite sex. He had, Adriana had wept on more than one occasion, thrown them out without a penny—so was it any wonder that she sometimes needed a little alcohol and a few substances to help her get by?

So many things for which Giancarlo had never forgiven his father…

He had stood on the sidelines and watched his delicate, spoilt mother—without any qualifications to speak of, always reliant on her beauty—demean herself by taking lover after lover, searching for the one who might want her enough to stick around. By the time she had died she had been a pathetic shadow of her former self.

'You have no idea of what my life was like, or what my mother's life was like,' Giancarlo framed icily. 'Perhaps my father has mellowed. Ill health has a habit of making servants of us all. However, I'm not interested in building bridges. Is that why he sent you here—because he's now an old man and he wants my forgiveness before he shuffles off this mortal coil?' He gave a bark of cynical, contemptuous laughter. 'I don't think so.'

She had continued playing with the handkerchief, twisting it between her fingers. Giancarlo thought that when it came to messengers, his father could not have been more calculating in his choice. The woman was a picture of teary-eyed incomprehension. Anyone would be forgiven for thinking that she worked for a saint, instead of for the man who had made his mother's life a living hell.

His sharp eyes narrowed and focused, taking in the details of her appearance. Her clothes were a fashion disaster—trousers and a blouse in a strange, sickly shade of yellow, both of which would have been better suited to someone twice her age. Her hair seemed to be escaping from a sort of makeshift braid, and it was long—really long. Not at all like the snappy bobs he was accustomed to seeing on women. And it was curly. She was free of make-up and he was suddenly conscious of the fact that her skin was very smooth, satin smooth, and she had an amazing mouth—full, well-defined lips, slightly parted now to reveal pearly-white teeth as she continued to stare at him with disappointment and incredulity.

'I'm sorry you're still so bitter about the past,' she murmured quietly. 'But he would really like to see you. Why is it too late to mend bridges? It would mean the world to him.'

'So have you managed to see anything of our beautiful city?'

'What? No. No, I've come directly here. Look, is there anything I can do or say to convince you to…to come back with me?'

'You have got to be kidding, haven't you? I mean, even if I were suddenly infused with a burning desire to become a prodigal son, do you really imagine that I would be able to drop everything, pack a bag and hop on the nearest train for Lake Como? Surprise, surprise—I have an empire to run.'

'Yes, but…'

'I'm a very busy man, Miss Rossi, and I have already allotted you a great deal of my very valuable time. Now, you could keep trying to convince me that I'm being a monster in not clapping my hands for joy that my father has suddenly decided to get in touch with me thanks to a bout of ill health…'

'You make it sound as though he's had a mild attack of flu! He's suffered a very serious *heart attack.*'

'For which I am truly sorry.' Giancarlo extended his arms wide in a gesture of such phoney sympathy that Caroline had to clench her fists to stop herself from smacking him. 'As I would be on learning of any stranger's brush with death. But, alas, you're going to have to go back empty-handed.'

Defeated, Caroline stood up and reached down for her suitcase.

'Where are you staying?' Giancarlo asked with scrupulous politeness as he watched the slump of her shoulders. God, had the old man really thought that there would be no consequences to pay for the destructive way he had treated his wife? He was as rich as they came and yet, according to Adriana, he had employed the best lawyers in the land to ensure that she received the barest of settlements, accessed through a trustee who had made sure the basics, the *absolute* basics, were paid for, and a meagre allowance handed over to her, like a child being given pocket money, scarcely enough to provide any standard of living. He had often wondered, over the years, whether his mother would have been as desperate to find love if she had been left sufficient money to meet her requirements.

Caroline wearily told him, although she knew full well that he didn't give a damn where she was staying. He just wanted her out of his office. She would be returning having failed. Of course, Alberto would be far too proud to do anything other than shrug his shoulders and say something about having tried, but she would know the truth. She would know that he would be gutted.

'Well, you make sure you try the food market at the Rinascente. You'll enjoy it. Tremendous views. And, of course, the shopping there is good as well.'

'I hate shopping.' Caroline came to a stop in front of the office door and turned around to find that he was virtually on top of her, towering a good eight or nine inches above her and even more intimidating this close up than he had been sitting safely behind his desk or lounging by the window.

The sun glinted from behind, picking out the striking angles of his face and rendering them more scarily beautiful. He had the most amazing eyelashes, long, lush and dark, the sort of eyelashes that most women could only ever have achieved with the help of tons of mascara.

She felt a sickening jolt somewhere in the region of her stomach and was suddenly and uncomfortably aware of her breasts, too big for her height, now sensitive, tingly and weighty as he stared down at her. Her hands wanted to flutter to the neckline of her blouse and draw the lapels tightly together. She flushed with embarrassment; how could she have forgotten that she was the ugly duckling?

'And I don't want to be having this polite conversation with you,' she breathed in a husky, defiant undertone.

'Come again?'

'I'm sorry your parents got divorced, and I'm really sorry that it left such a mark on you, but I think it's horrible that you won't give your father another chance. How do you know exactly what happened between your parents? You were only a child. Your father's ill and you'd rather carry on holding a grudge than try and make the most of the time you have left of him. He might die tomorrow, for all we know!'

That short speech took a lot out of her. She wasn't usually defiant, but this man set her teeth on edge. 'How can you say that, even if you were interested in meeting him, you couldn't possibly get away because you're too important?'

'I said that I have an empire to run.'

'It's the same thing!' She was shaking all over, like a leaf, but she looked up at him with un-flinching determination, chin jutting out, her brown eyes, normally mild, flashing fire. 'Okay, I'm not going to see you again...' Caroline drew in a deep breath and impatiently swept her dis-obedient hair from away her face. 'So I can be re-ally honest with you.'

Giancarlo moved to lounge against the door, arms folded, an expression of lively curiosity on his face. Her cheeks were flushed and her eyes glittered. She was a woman in a rage and he was getting the impression that this was a woman who didn't *do* rages. God, wasn't this turning into one hell of a day?

'I don't suppose *anyone* is really ever honest with you, are they?' She looked around the of-fice, with its mega-expensive fittings, ancient rug, worn bookshelves, the painting on the wall—the only modern one she had glimpsed, which looked vaguely familiar. Who was really ever that honest with someone as wealthy as he appeared to be, as good-looking as he was? He had the arrogance of a man who always got exactly what he wanted.

'It's useful when my man who handles my stocks

and shares tells me what he thinks. Although, in fairness, I usually know more than he does. I should get rid of him but—' he shrugged with typical Italian nonchalance '—we go back a long way.'

He shot her a smile that was so unconsciously charming that Caroline was nearly knocked backwards by the force of it. It was like being in a dark room only to be suddenly dazzled by a ray of blistering sunshine. Which didn't distract her from the fact that he refused to see his father, a sick and possibly dying old man. Refused to bury the hatchet, whatever the consequences. Charming smiles counted for nothing when it came to the bigger picture!

'I'm glad you think that this is a big joke,' she said tightly. 'I'm glad that you can laugh about it, but you know what? I feel *sorry* for you! You might think that the only thing that matters is all…all *this*…but none of this counts when it comes to relationships and family. I think you're… you're *arrogant* and *high-handed* and making a huge mistake!'

Outburst over, Caroline yanked open the office door to a surprised Elena, who glanced at her with

consternation before looking behind to where her
boss, the man who never lost his steely grip on
his emotions, was staring at the small, departing
brunette with the incredulous expression of someone who has been successfully tackled when least
expecting it.

'Stop staring,' Giancarlo said. He shook his
head, dazed, and then offered his secretary a wry
grin. 'We all lose our cool sometimes.'

CHAPTER TWO

MILAN was a diverse and beautiful city. There were sufficient museums, galleries, basilicas and churches to keep any tourist busy. The Galleria Vittorio was a splendid and elegant arcade, stuffed with cafés and shops. Caroline knew all this because the following day—her last day before she returned to Alberto, when she would have to admit failure—she made sure to read all the literature on a city which she might not visit again. It was tarnished with the miserable experience of having met Giancarlo De Vito.

The more Caroline thought about him, the more arrogant and unbearable he seemed. She just couldn't find a single charitable thing to credit him with. Alberto would be waiting for her, expecting to see her arrive with his son and, failing that, he would be curious for details. Would she be honest and admit to him that she had found his sinfully beautiful son loathsome and overbearing?

Would any parent, even an estranged parent, be grateful for information like that?

She looked down to where her ice-cold glass of lemonade was slowly turning warm in the searing heat. She had dutifully spent two hours walking around the Duomo, admiring the stained-glass windows, the impressive statues of saints and the extravagant carvings. But her heart hadn't been in it, and now here she was, in one of the little cafés, which outside on a hot summer day was packed to the rafters with tourists sitting and lazily people-watching.

Her thoughts were in turmoil. With an impatient sigh, she glanced down at her watch, wondering how she would fill the remainder of her day, and was unaware of the shadow looming over her until she heard Giancarlo's velvety, familiar voice which had become embedded in her head like an irritating burr.

'You lied to me.'

Caroline looked up, shading her eyes from the glare of the sun, at about the same time as a wad of papers landed on the small circular table in front of her.

She was so shocked to see him towering over

her, blocking out the sun like a dark avenging angel, that she half-spilled her drink in her confusion.

'What are you doing here? And how did you find me?' Belatedly she noticed the papers on the table. 'And what's all that stuff?'

'We need to have a little chat and this place isn't doing it for me.'

Caroline felt her heart lift a little. Maybe he was reconsidering his original stance. Maybe, just maybe, he had seen the light and was now prepared to let bygones be bygones. She temporarily forgot his ominous opening words and the mysterious stack of papers in front of her.

'Of course!' She smiled brightly and then cleared her throat when there was no reciprocal smile. 'I… You haven't said how you managed to find me. Where are we going? Am I supposed to bring all this stuff with me?'

Presumably, yes, as he spun round on his heels and was scouring the *piazza* through narrowed eyes. Did he notice the interested stares he was garnering from the tourists, particularly the women? Or was he immune to that sort of attention?

Caroline grabbed the papers and scrambled to follow him as he strode away from the café through a series of small roads, leaving the crush of tourists behind.

Today, she had worn the only other outfit she had brought with her, a summer dress with small buttons down the front. Because it left her shoulders bare, and because she was so acutely conscious of her generous breasts, she had a thin pink cardigan slung loosely over her—which wasn't exactly practical, given the weather, but without it she felt too exposed and self-conscious.

With the ease of someone who lived in the city, he weaved his way through the busier areas until they were finally at a small café tucked away from the tourist hotspots, although even here the ancient architecture, the charming square with its sixteenth-century well, the engravings on some of the façades, were all photo opportunities.

She dithered behind him, feeling a bit like a spare part as he spoke in rapid Italian to a short, plump man whom she took to be the owner of the café. Then he motioned her inside where it was blessedly cool and relatively empty.

'You can sit,' Giancarlo said irritably when she

continued to hover by the table. What did his father see in the woman? He barely remembered
Alberto, but one thing he *did* remember was that
he had not been the most docile person in the
world. If his mother had been a difficult woman,
then she had found her match in her much older
husband. What changes had the years wrought,
if Alberto was happy to work with someone who
had to be the most background woman he had
ever met? And once again she was in an outfit
that would have been more suitable on a woman
twice her age. Truly the English hadn't got a clue
when it came to fashion.

He found himself appraising her body and then,
surprisingly, lingering on her full breasts pushing
against the thin cotton dress, very much in evi-
dence despite the washed-out cardigan she had
draped over her shoulders.

'You never said how you managed to find me,'
Caroline repeated a little breathlessly as she slid
into the chair opposite him.

She shook away the giddy, drowning feeling she
had when she looked too hard at him. Something
about his animal sex-appeal was horribly unset-

tling, too hard to ignore and not quite what she was used to.

'You told me where you were staying. I went there first thing this morning and was told by the receptionist that you'd left for the Duomo. It was just a question of time before you followed the herd to one of the cafés outside.'

'So…have you had a rethink?' Caroline asked hopefully. She wondered how it was that he could look so cool and urbane in his cream trousers and white shirt while the rest of the population seemed to be slowly dissolving under the summer sun.

'Have a look at the papers in front of you.'

Caroline dutifully flicked through them. 'I'm sorry, I have no idea what these are—and I'm not very good with numbers.' She had wisely tied her hair back today but still some curling strands found their way to her cheeks and she absent-mindedly tucked them behind her ears while she continued to frown at the pages and pages of bewildering columns and numbers in front of her, finally giving up.

'After I saw you I decided to run a little check on Alberto's company accounts. You're looking at my findings.'

'I don't understand why you've shown me this. I don't know anything about Alberto's financial affairs. He doesn't talk about that at all.'

'Funny, but I never thought him particularly shy when it came to money. In fact, I would say that he's always had his finger on the button in that area.'

'How would you know, when you haven't seen him for over a decade?'

Giancarlo thought of the way Alberto had short changed his mother and his lips curled cynically. 'Let's move away from that contentious area, shall we? And let's focus on one or two interesting things I unearthed.' He sat back as cold drinks were placed in front of them, along with a plate of delicate little *tortas* and pastries. 'By the way, help yourself...' He gestured to the dish of pastries and cakes and was momentarily sidetracked when she pulled her side plate in front of her and piled a polite mound, but a mound nevertheless, of the delicacies on it.

'You're actually going to eat all of those?' he heard himself ask, fascinated against his will.

'I know, I shouldn't really. But I'm starving.' Caroline sighed at the diet which she had been planning for ages and which had yet to get under-way. 'You don't mind, do you? I mean…they're not just here for *show*, are they?'

'No, *di niente*.' He sat back and watched as she nibbled her way through the pastries, politely leaving one, licking the sweet crumbs off her fingers with enjoyment. A rare sight. The stick-thin women he dated pushed food round their plates and would have recoiled in horror at the thought of eating anything as fattening as a pastry.

Of course, he should be getting on with what he wanted to say, but he had been thrown off course and he still was when she shot him an apologetic smile. There was an errant crumb at the side of her mouth and just for an instant he had an over-whelming urge to brush it off. Instead, he gestured to her mouth with his hand.

'I always have big plans for going on a diet.' Caroline blushed. 'Once or twice I actually did, but diets are deadly. Have you ever been on one? No, I bet you haven't. Well, salads are all well and good, but just try making them interesting. I guess I just really love food.'

'That's…unusual. In a woman. Most of the

women I meet do their best to avoid the whole eating experience.'

Of course he would be the type who only associated with model types, Caroline thought sourly. Thin, leggy women who weighed nothing. She wished she hadn't indulged her sweet tooth. Not that it mattered because, although he might be good-looking—well, staggering, really—he wasn't the sort of man she would ever go for. So what did it matter if he thought that she was overweight and greedy into the bargain?

'You were saying something about Alberto's financial affairs?' She glanced down at her watch, because why on earth should he have the monopoly on precious time? 'It's just that I leave tomorrow morning and I want to make sure that I get through as much as possible before I go.'

Giancarlo was, for once in his life, virtually lost for words. Was she *hurrying him along*?

'I think,' he asserted without inflection, 'that your plans will have to take a back seat until I'm finished.'

'You haven't told me whether you've decided to put the past behind you and accompany me back to Lake Como.' She didn't know why she was bothering to ask the question because it was obvious that he had no such intention.

'So you came here to see me for the sole purpose of masterminding a jolly reunion...'

'It wasn't *my* idea.'

'Immaterial. Getting back to the matter in hand, the fact is that Alberto's company accounts show a big, gaping black hole.'

Caroline frowned because she genuinely had no idea what he was talking about.

'*Si,*' Giancarlo imparted without a shade of regret as he continued to watch her so carefully that she could feel the colour mounting in her cheeks. 'He has been leaking money for the past ten years but recently it's become something more akin to a haemorrhage...'

Caroline gasped and stared at him in sudden consternation. 'Oh my goodness... Do you think that that's why he had the heart attack?'

'I beg your pardon?'

'I didn't think he took an active interest in what happened in the company. I mean, he's been pretty much a recluse since I came to live with him.'

'Which would be how long ago?'

'Several months. Originally, I only intended to

come for a few weeks, but we got along so well and there were so many things he wanted me to do that I found myself staying on.' She fixed anxious brown eyes on Giancarlo, who seemed sublimely immune to an ounce of compassion at the news he had casually delivered.

'Are you…are you sure you've got your facts right?'

'I'm never wrong,' he said drily. 'It's possible that Alberto hasn't played an active part in running his company for some time now. It's more than possible that he's been merrily living off the dividends and foolishly imagining that his investments are paying off.'

'And what if he only recently found out?' Caroline cried, determined not to become too over-emotional in front of a man who, she knew, would see emotion in a woman as repellent. Besides, she had cried on him yesterday. She still had the handkerchief to prove it. Once had been bad enough but twice would be unforgivable.

'Do you think that that might have contributed to his heart attack? Do you think that he became so stressed that it affected his health?' Horribly rattled at that thought, she distractedly helped herself to the last pastry lying uneaten on her plate.

'No one can ever accuse me of being a gullible man, Signorina Rossi.' Giancarlo was determined to stick to the script. 'One lesson I've learnt in life is that, when it comes to money, there will always be people around who are more than happy to scheme their way into getting their hands on some of it.'

'Yes. Yes, I suppose so. Whatever. Poor Alberto. He never mentioned a word and yet he must have been so worried. Imagine having to deal with that on your own.'

'Yes. Poor Alberto. Still, whilst poring over these findings, it occurred to me that your mission here might very well have been twofold...'

'The doctor said that stress can cause all sorts of health problems.'

'Focus, signorina!'

Caroline fell silent and looked at him. The sun wafting through the pane of glass made his hair look all the more glossy. She vaguely noticed the way it curled at the collar of his shirt. Somehow, it made him look very exotic and very European.

'Now are you with me?'

'There's no need to talk down to me!'

'There's every need. You have the most wandering mind of anyone I've ever met.'

Caroline shot him a look of simmering resentment and added 'rude' to the increasingly long list of things she didn't like about him.

'And you are the *rudest* person I've ever met in my entire life!'

Giancarlo couldn't remember the last time anyone had ever dared to insult him to his face. He didn't think it had ever happened. Rather than be sidetracked, however, he chose to overlook her offensive remark.

'It occurred to me that my father's health, if your story about his heart attack is to be believed, might not be the primary reason for your visit to Milan.'

'If my story is to be believed?' She shook her head with a puzzled frown. 'Why would I lie about something like that?'

'I'll answer a question with a question—why would my father suddenly choose *now* to seek me out? He had more than one opportunity to get in touch. He never bothered. So why now? Shall I put forward a theory? He's wised up to the fact that his wealth has disappeared down the proverbial tubes and has sent you to check out the situation. Perhaps he told you that, if I seemed amenable to the idea of meeting up, you might mention the possibility of a loan?'

Shocked and disturbed by Giancarlo's free-wheeling assumptions and cynical, half-baked misunderstandings, Caroline didn't know where to begin. She just stared at him as the colour drained away from her face. She wasn't normally given to anger, but right now she had to stop herself from picking her plate up and smashing it over his arrogant head.

'So maybe I wasn't entirely accurate when I accused you of lying to me. Maybe it would be more accurate to say that you were conveniently economical with the full truth...'

'I can't believe I'm hearing you say these things! How could you accuse your own father of trying to squeeze money out of you?'

Giancarlo flushed darkly under her steady, clear-eyed, incredulous gaze. 'Like I said, money has a nasty habit of bringing out the worst in people. Do you know that it's a given fact that the second someone wins a lottery, they suddenly discover that they have a hell of a lot more close friends and relatives than they ever imagined?'

'Alberto hasn't sent me here on a mission to get money out of you or…or to ask you for a loan!'

'Are you telling me that he had no idea that I was now a wealthy man?'

'That's not the point.' She remembered Alberto's statement that Giancarlo had made something of himself.

'No? You're telling me that there's no link between one semi-bankrupt father who hasn't been on the scene in nearly two decades and his sudden, inexplicable desire to meet the rich son he was happy to kick out of his house once upon a time?'

'Yes!'

'Well, if you really believe that, if you're not in cahoots with Alberto, then you must be incredibly naïve.'

'I feel very sorry for you, Signor De Vito.'

'Call me Giancarlo. I feel as though we almost know each other. Certainly no one can compete with you when it comes to delivering offensive remarks. You are in a league of your own.'

Caroline flushed because she was not given to

being offensive. She was placid and easy-going by nature. However, she was certainly not going to apologise for speaking her mind to Giancarlo.

'You are pretty offensive as well,' she retaliated quietly. 'You've just accused me of being a liar. Maybe in *your* world you can never trust anyone...'

'I think it's fair to say that trust is a much over-rated virtue. I have a great deal of money. I've learnt to protect myself, simple as that.' He gave an elegant shrug, dismissing the topic. But Caroline wasn't quite ready to let the matter drop, to allow him to continue believing, unchallenged, that he had somehow been targeted by Alberto. She wouldn't let him walk away thinking the worst of either of them.

'I don't think that trust is an over-rated virtue. I told you that I feel sorry for you and I really do.' She had to steel herself to meet and hold the dark, forbidding depths of his icy eyes. 'I think it's sad to live in a world where you can never allow yourself to believe the best in other people. How can you ever be happy if you're always thinking that the people around you are out to take advantage of you? How can you ever be happy if you don't have faith in the people who are close to you?'

Giancarlo very nearly burst out laughing at that. What planet was this woman from? It was a cutthroat world out there and it became even more cutthroat when money and finances were involved. You had to keep your friends close and your enemies a whole lot closer in order to avoid the risk of being knifed in the back.

'Don't go getting evangelical on me,' he murmured drily and he noted the pink colour rise to her cheeks. 'You're blushing,' he surprised himself by saying.

'Because I'm angry!' But she put her hands to her face and glared at him. 'You're so…so *superior*! What sort of people do you mix with that you would suspect them of trying to use you for what you can give them? I didn't know anything about you when I agreed to come here. I didn't know that you had lots of money. I just knew that Alberto was ill and he wanted to make his peace with you.'

The oddest thing seemed to be happening. Giancarlo could feel himself getting distracted. Was it because of the way those tendrils of curly hair were wisping against her face? Or was it because her anger made her almond-shaped eyes gleam like a furious spitting cat's? Or maybe it was the fact that, when she leant forward like that, the weight and abundance of her breasts brushing against the small table acted like a magnet to his wandering eyes.

It was a strange sensation to experience this slight loss of self-control because it never happened in his dealings with women. And he was a connoisseur when it came to the opposite sex. Without a trace of vanity, he knew that he possessed a combination of looks, power and influence that most women found an irresistible aphrodisiac. Right now, he had only recently broken off a six-month relationship with a model whose stunning looks had graced the covers of a number of magazines. She had begun to make noises about 'taking things further'; had started mentioning friends and relatives who were thinking of tying the knot; had begun to show an unhealthy interest in the engagement-ring section of expensive jewellery shops.

Giancarlo had no interest in going down the matrimonial path. There were two vital lessons he felt he had taken away from his parents: the first was that there was no such thing as a happy-ever-after. The second was that it was very easy for a woman to turn from angel to shrew. The loving woman who was happy to accommodate on every level quickly became the demanding, needy harridan who needed reassurance and attention round the clock.

He had watched his mother contrive to play the perfect partner on so many occasions that he had lost count. He had watched her perform her magic with whatever man happened to be the flavour of the day for a while, had watched her bat her eyelashes and flutter her eyes—but then, when things began winding down, he had seen how she had changed from eager to desperate, from hard-to-get to clingy and dependent. The older she had got, the more pitiful a sight she had made.

Of course, he was a red-blooded man with an extremely healthy libido, but as far as Giancarlo was concerned work was a far better bet when it came to reliability. Women, enjoyable as they might be, became instantly expendable the second they began thinking that they could change him.

He had never let any woman get under his skin

and he was surprised now to find his thoughts drifting ever so slightly from the matter at hand.

He had confronted her, having done some background research, simply to have his suspicions confirmed. It had been a simple exercise in proving to her—and via her to Alberto—that he wasn't a mug who could be taken for a ride. At which point, his plan had been to walk away, warning guns sounding just in case they were tempted to try a second approach.

From the very second Caroline had shown up unannounced in his office, he had not allowed a shred of sentiment to colour his judgement. Bitter memories of the stories handed down to him from his mother still cast a long shadow. The truth he had seen with his very own eyes—the way her lack of any kind of robust financial settlement from a man who would have been very wealthy at the time had influenced her behaviour patterns—could not be overlooked.

'You must get bored out there,' Giancarlo heard himself remark when he should have really been thinking of concluding their conversation so that he could return to the various meetings waiting for him back at the office. Without taking his eyes off her, he flicked a finger and more cold drinks were brought to their table.

Caroline could no more follow this change in the conversation than she could have dealt with a snarling crocodile suddenly deciding to smile and offer her a cup of tea. She looked at him warily and wondered whether this was a roundabout lead-up to another scathing attack.

'Why are you interested?' she asked cautiously.

'Why not? It's not every day that a complete stranger waltzes into my office with a bombshell. Even if it turns out to be a bombshell that's easy to defuse. Also—and I'll be completely honest on this score—you don't strike me as the sort of person capable of dealing with the man I remember as being my father.'

Caroline was drawn into the conversation against her will. 'What do you remember?' she asked hesitantly. With another cold drink in front of her, the sight of those remaining pastries was awfully tempting. As though reading her mind, Giancarlo ordered a few more, different ones this time, smiling as they were placed in front of her.

He was amused to watch the struggle on her face as she looked down at them.

'What do I remember of my father? Now, let's think about this. Domineering. Frequently ill-tempered. Controlling. In short, not the easiest person in the world.'

'Like you, in other words.'

Giancarlo's mouth tightened because this was an angle that had never occurred to him and he wasn't about to give it house-room now.

'Sorry. I shouldn't have said that.'

'No, you shouldn't, but I'm already getting used to the idea that you speak before you think. Something else I imagine Alberto would have found unacceptable.'

'I really don't like you *at all*,' Caroline said through gritted teeth. 'And I take back what I said. You're *nothing* like Alberto.'

'I'm thrilled to hear that. So, enlighten me.' He felt a twinge of intense curiosity about this man who had been so thoroughly demonised by his ex-wife.

'Well.' Caroline smiled slowly and Giancarlo was amazed at how that slow, reluctant, suspicious smile altered the contours of her face, turning her into someone strangely beautiful in a lush, ripe way that was even more erotic, given the innocence of everything else about her. It put all sorts of crazy thoughts in his head, although the thoughts lasted only an instant, disappearing fast under the mental discipline that was so much part and parcel of his personality.

'He can be grumpy. He's very grumpy now because he hates being told what he can and can't eat and what time he has to go to bed. He hates me helping him physically, so he's employed a local woman, a nurse from the hospital, to help him instead, and I'm constantly having to tell him that he's got to be less bossy and critical of her.

'He was very polite when I first arrived. I think he knew that he was doing my dad a favour, but he figured that he would only have to be on good behaviour for a few weeks. I don't think he knew what to do with me, to start with. He's not been used to company. He wasn't comfortable making eye contact, but none of that lasted too long. We discovered that we shared so many interests— books, old movies, the garden. In fact, the garden has been invaluable now that Alberto is recovering. Every day we go down to the pond just beyond the walled rose-garden. We sit in the folly, read a bit, chat a bit. He likes me to read to him even though he's forever telling me that I need to put more expression in my voice… I guess all that's going to have to go…'

Giancarlo, who hadn't thought of what he had left behind for a very long time, had a vivid memory of that pond and of the folly, a weird gazebo-style creation with a very comfortable bench inside where he likewise had enjoyed whiling away his time during the long summer months when he had been on holiday. He shook away the memory as if clearing cobwebs from a cupboard that hadn't been opened for a long time.

'What do you mean that you guess that's all "going to have to go"?'

Caroline settled worried eyes on his face. For someone who was clearly so intelligent, she was surprised that he didn't seem to follow her. Then she realised that she couldn't very well explain without risking another attack on Alberto's scruples.

'Nothing,' she mumbled when his questioning silence threatened to become too uncomfortable.

'Tut tut. Are you going to get tongue-tied on me?'

The implication being that she talked far too much, Caroline concluded, hurt.

'What do you mean? And don't bother trying to be coy. It doesn't suit you.'

Caroline didn't think she could feel more loathing for another human being if she tried.

'Well, if Alberto has run into financial difficulties, then he's not going to be able to maintain the house, is he? I mean, it's enormous. Right now, a lot of it isn't used, but he would still have to sell it. And please don't tell me that this is a ploy to try and get money out of you. It isn't.' She sighed in weary resignation. 'I don't know why I'm telling you that. You won't believe me anyway.' Suddenly, she was anxious to leave, to get back to the house on the lake, although she had no idea what she was going to do once she got there. Confront Alberto with his problems? Risk jeopardising his fragile health by piling more stress on his shoulders?

'I'm not even sure your father knows the truth of the situation,' she said miserably. 'I'm certain he would have mentioned something to me.'

'Why would he? You've been around for five seconds. I suggest the first person on his list of confidants would probably have been his accountant.'

'Maybe he's told Father Rafferty. I could go and see him at the church and find out if he knows about any of this. That would be the best thing, because Father Rafferty would be able to put everything into perspective. He's very practical and upbeat.'

'Father Rafferty…?'

'Alberto attends mass at the local church every Sunday. Has done for a long time, I gather. He and Father Rafferty have become close friends. I think your father likes Father Rafferty's Irish sense of humour—and the odd glass of whisky. I should go. All of this…'

'Is probably very unsettling, and probably not what you contemplated when you first decided to come over to Italy.'

'I don't mind!' Caroline was quick to reply. She bit back the temptation to tell him that *someone* had to be there for Alberto.

Giancarlo was realising that his original assumption, which had made perfect sense at the time, had been perhaps a little too hasty. The woman was either an excellent, Oscar-winning actress or else she had been telling the truth all along: her visit had not been instigated for financial purposes.

Now his brain was engaged on a different path; he sat back and looked at her as he stroked his chin thoughtfully with one long, brown finger.

'I expect this nurse he's hired is a private nurse?'

Caroline hadn't given that a second's thought, but now she blanched. How much would that be costing? And didn't it prove that Alberto had no idea of the state of his finances? Why, if he did know, would he be spending money on hiring a private nurse who would be costing him an arm and a leg?

'And naturally he must be paying *you*,' Giancarlo continued remorselessly. 'How much?' He named a figure that was so ridiculously high that Caroline burst out laughing. She laughed until she felt tears come to her eyes. It was as though she had found a sudden outlet for her stressful, frantic thoughts and her body was reacting of its own volition, even though Giancarlo was now looking at her with the perplexed expression of someone dealing with a complete idiot.

'Sorry.' She hiccupped her way back to some level of seriousness, although she could still feel her mirth lurking close to the surface. 'You've got to be kidding. Take that figure and maybe divide it by four.'

'Don't be ridiculous. No one could survive on that.'

'But I never came here for the money,' Caroline explained patiently. 'I came here to improve my Italian. Alberto was doing me a favour by taking me in. I don't have to pay for food and I don't pay rent. When I return to England, the fact that I will be able to communicate in another language will be a great help to me when it comes to getting a job. Why are you staring at me like that?'

'So it doesn't bother you that you wouldn't be able to have much of a life given that you're paid next to nothing?' *Cheap labour,* Giancarlo thought. *Now, why am I not surprised?* A specialised nurse would hardly donate her services through the goodness of her heart, but a young, clearly inexperienced girl? Why not take advantage? Oh, the old man knew the state of his finances, all right, whatever she exclaimed to the contrary.

'I don't mind. I've never been fussed about money.'

'Guess what?' Giancarlo signalled to the waiter for the bill. When Caroline looked at her watch, it was to find that the time had galloped by. She hadn't even been aware of it passing, even though, disliking him as she did, she should have been counting every agonising minute.

'What?'

'Consider your little mission a success. I think it's time, after all, to return home…'

CHAPTER THREE

GIANCARLO'S last view of his father's house, as he had twisted around in the back of the car, while in the front his mother had sat in stony silence without a backward glance, was of lush gardens and the vast stone edifice which comprised the back of the house. The front of the house sat grandly on the western shores of the lake, perfect positioning for a view of deep blue water, as still as a sheet of glass, that was breathtakingly beautiful.

It was unsettling to be returning now, exactly one week after Caroline had left, seemingly transported with excitement at the fact that she had managed to persuade him to accept the supposed olive-branch that had been extended.

If she was of the opinion that all was joyful in the land of reconciliation, then Giancarlo was equally and coldly reserved about sharing any such optimism. He was under no illusions when it came to human nature. The severity of Alberto's heart attack was open to debate and Giancarlo, for one, was coolly prepared for a man in fairly robust health who may or may not have persuaded a very gullible Caroline otherwise to suit his own purposes. His memories of his father were of a towering man, greatly into discipline and without an emotional bone in his body. He couldn't conceive of him being diminished by ill health, although rapidly disappearing funds might well have played a part in lowering his spirits.

The super-fast sports car had eaten up the miles of motorway and only now, as he slowed to drive through the picturesque towns and villages on the way to his father's house, were vague recollections beginning to surface.

He had forgotten how charming this area was. Lake Como, the third largest and the deepest of the Italian lakes, was picture-postcard perfect, a lush, wealthy area with elegant villas, manicured gardens, towns and villages with cobbled streets and *piazzas* dotted with Romanesque churches and very expensive hotels and restaurants which attracted the more discerning tourist.

He felt a pleasing sense of satisfaction.

This was a homecoming on *his* terms, just

the way he liked it. A more in-depth perusal of Alberto's finances had shown a company torn apart by the ravaging effects of an unprecedented economic recession, mismanagement and an unwillingness to move with the times and invest in new markets.

Giancarlo smiled grimly to himself. He had never considered himself a vengeful person but the realisation that he could take over his father's company, rescue the old man and thereby level the scales of justice was a pleasing one. Really, what more bitter pill could his father ever swallow than know that he was indebted, literally, to the son he had turned his back on?

He hadn't mentioned a word of this to Caroline when they had parted company. For a few minutes, Giancarlo found himself distracted by thoughts of the diminutive brunette. She was flaky as hell; unbelievably emotional and prone to tears at the drop of a hat; jaw-droppingly forthright and, frankly, left him speechless. But, as he got closer and closer to the place he had once called his home, he realised that she had managed to get under his skin in a way that was uniquely irritating. In fact, he had never devoted this much time to thinking about any one woman, but that, he reasoned sensibly, was because this particular woman had entered his life in a singularly weird way.

Never again would he rule out the unexpected. Just when you thought you had everything in control, something came along to pull the rug from under your feet.

In this instance, it wasn't all bad. He fiddled with the radio, got to a station he liked and relaxed to enjoy the scenery and the pleasing prospect of what lay ahead.

He gave no house room to nerves. He was on a high, in fact, fuelled by the self-righteous notion of the wheel having turned full circle. Yes, he was curious to reacquaint himself with Alberto, but over the years he had heard so many things about him that he almost felt as though there was nothing left to know. The steady drip, drip, drip of information from a young age had eroded his natural inclination to question.

If anything, he liked to think that Alberto would be the one consumed by nerves. His business was failing and sooner or later, ill health or no ill health, Giancarlo was certain that his father would turn the conversation around to money. Maybe he would try and entice him into some kind of investment. Maybe he would just ditch his pride and ask outright for a loan of some sort. Either approach was possible. Giancarlo relished the prospect of being able to confirm that money would indeed be forthcoming. Wasn't he magnanimous even though, all things considered, he had no reason to be? But a price would have to be paid. He would make his father's company his own. He would take it over lock, stock and barrel. Yes, his father's financial security would rest on the generosity of his disowned son.

He intended to stay at the villa just long enough to convey that message. A couple of days at most. Thereafter it would be enough to know that he had done what he had to do.

He didn't anticipate having anything to say of interest to the old man. Why should he? They would be two strangers, relieved to part company once the nitty-gritty had been sorted out.

He was so wrapped up in his thoughts that he very nearly missed the turning to the villa. This side of the lake was famous for its magnificent villas, most of them eighteenth-century extravaganzas, a few of which had been turned into hotels over the years.

His father's villa was by no means the largest but it was still an impressive old place, approached through forbidding iron gates and a long drive which was surrounded on both sides by magnificent gardens.

He remembered the layout of these glorious spreading lawns more than he had anticipated. To the right, there was the bank of trees in which he had used to play as a child. To the left, the stone wall was barely visible behind rows upon rows of rhododendrons and azaleas, a vibrant wash of colour as bright and as dramatic as a child's painting.

He slowed the car in the circular courtyard, killed the engine and popped the boot, which was just about big enough to fit his small leather overnight case—and, of course, his computer bag in which resided all the necessary documents he would need so that he could begin the takeover process he had in mind for his father's company.

He was an imposing sight. From her bedroom window, which overlooked the courtyard, Caroline felt a sudden sick flutter of nerves.

Over the past seven days, she had done her best to play down the impact he had made on her. He wasn't *that* tall, *that* good-looking or *that* arrogant, she convinced herself. She had been rattled when she had finally located him and her nerves had thrown everything out of perspective.

Unfortunately, staring down at Giancarlo as he emerged from his sports car, wearing dark sunglasses and walking round to swing two cases out of the miniscule boot of his car, she realised that he really *was* as unbelievably forbidding as she had remembered.

She literally flew down the corridor, took the staircase two steps at a time and reached the sitting-room at the back of the house, breathless.

'He's here!'

Alberto was sitting in a chair by the big bay window that had a charming view of the gardens stretching down to the lake, which was dotted with little boats.

'Anyone would think the Pope was paying a visit. Calm down, girl! Your colour's up.'

'You're going to be nice, aren't you, Alberto?'

'I'm always nice. You just fuss too much, get yourself worked up over small things—it's not good for you. Now, off you go and let the boy in before he climbs back into his car and drives away. And on your way you can tell that nurse of yours that I'm having a glass of whisky before dinner. Whether she likes it or not!'

'I'll do no such thing, Alberto De Vito. If you want to disobey doctor's orders, then you can tell Tessa yourself—and I would love to see how she takes that.' She grinned fondly at the old man, who was backlit by the evening sun glinting through the window. Having met Giancarlo, she found the similarities between them striking. Both had the same proud, aristocratic features and the long, lean lines of natural athletes. Of course, Alberto was elderly now, but it was easy to see that he must have been as striking as his son in his youth.

'Oh, stop that endless chattering, woman, and run along.' He waved her off and Caroline, steadying her nerves, got to the front door just as the doorbell chimed.

She smoothed nervous hands along her skirt, a black maxi in stretch cotton which she wore with a loose-fitting top and, of course, the ubiquitous cardigan, although at least here it was more appropriate thanks to the cooling breeze that blew off the lake.

She pulled open the door and her mouth went dry. In a snug-fitting cream polo-necked shirt and a pair of tan trousers with very expensive-looking loafers, he was every inch the impeccably dressed Italian. He looked as though he had come straight from a fashion shoot until he raised one sardonic eyebrow and said coolly, 'Were you waiting by the window?'

Remembering that she *had*, actually, been at her window when his car had pulled into the court-yard, Caroline straightened her spine and cleared her throat.

'Of course I wasn't! Although I *was* tempted, just in case you didn't show up.' She stood aside; Giancarlo took a step through the front door and confronted the house in which he had spent the first twelve years of his life. It had changed re-markably little. The hall was a vast expanse of marble, in the centre of which a double staircase spiralled in opposing directions to meet on the impressive galleried landing above. On either side of the hall, a network of rooms radiated like ten-tacles on an octopus.

Now that he was back, he could place every room in his head: the various reception rooms; the imposing study from which he had always been banned; the dining-room in which portraits of deceased family members glared down at the assembled diners; the gallery in which were hung paintings of great value, another room from which he had been banned.

'Why wouldn't I show up?' Giancarlo turned to face her. She looked more at home here, less ill at ease, which was hardly surprising, he supposed. Her hair which she had attempted to tie back in Milan was loose, and it flowed over her shoulders and down her back in a tangle of curls, dark brown streaked with caramel where the sun had lightened it.

'You might have had a change of heart,' Caroline admitted in a harried voice, because yet again those dark, cloaked eyes on her were doing weird things to her tummy. 'I mean, you were so adamant that you didn't want to see your father and then all of a sudden you announced that you'd changed your mind. It didn't make sense. So I thought that maybe you might have changed your mind again.'

'Where are the staff?'

'I told you, most of the house is shut off. We have Tessa, the nurse who looks after Alberto. She lives on the premises, and two young girls take care of cleaning the house, but they live in the village. I'm glad you decided to come after all. Shall we go and meet your father? I guess you'll want to be with him on your own.'

'So that we can catch up? Exchange fond memories of the good old days?'

Caroline looked at him in dismay. There was no attempt to disguise the bitterness in his voice. Alberto rarely mentioned the past, and his memoirs, which had taken a back seat over the past few weeks, had mostly got to the state of fond reminiscing about his university days and the places he had travelled as a young man. But she could imagine that Alberto had not been the easiest of fathers. When Giancarlo had agreed to visit, she had naïvely assumed that he had been willing, finally, to overlook whatever mishaps had drastically torn them apart. Now, looking at him, she was uneasily aware that her simple conclusions might have been a little off the mark.

'Or even just agree to put the past behind you and move on,' Caroline offered helpfully.

Giancarlo sighed. Should he let her in to what he had planned? he wondered.

'Why don't you give me a little tour of the house before I meet my father?' he suggested. 'I want to get a feel of the old place. And there are a couple of things I want to talk to you about.'

'Things? What things?'

'If you don't fancy the full tour, you can show me to my bedroom. What I have to say won't take long.'

'I'll show you to your room,' she said stiffly. 'But first I'll go and tell Alberto where we are, so he doesn't worry.'

'Why would he worry?'

'He's been looking forward to seeing you.'

'I'm thinking I will be in my old room,' Giancarlo murmured. 'Left wing. Overlooking the side gardens?'

'The left wing's not really used now.' Making her mind up, she eyed his lack of luggage and began heading up the stairs. 'I'll take you up to where you'll be staying. If we're quick, I'm sure your father won't get too anxious. And you can tell me whatever it is you have to tell me.'

She could feel her heart beating like a sledge-hammer inside her as she preceded him up the grand staircase, turning left along the equally grand corridor, which was broad enough to house a *chaise longue* and various highly polished tables on which sat bowls of fresh flowers. Caroline had added that touch soon after she had come to live with Alberto and he had grumpily acquiesced, but not before informing her that flowers inside a house were a waste of time. Why bother when they would die within the week?

'Ah, the Green Room.' Giancarlo looked around him and saw the signs of disrepair. The room looked tired, the wallpaper still elegant but badly faded. The curtains he dimly remembered, although this was one of the many guest rooms into which he had seldom ventured. Nothing had been changed in over two decades. He dumped his overnight bag on the bed and walked across to the window to briefly look down at the exquisite walled garden, before turning to her.

'I feel I ought to tell you that my decision to come here wasn't entirely altruistic,' he told her bluntly. 'I wouldn't want you having any misplaced notions of emotional reunions, because if you have, then you're in for a crashing disappointment.'

'Not entirely altruistic?'

'Alberto's rocky financial situation has—how shall I put it?—delivered me the perfect opportunity to finally redress certain injustices.'

'What injustices?'

'Nothing you need concern yourself with. Suffice to say that Alberto will not have to fear that the banks are going to repossess this house and all its contents.'

'This house was going to be repossessed?'

'Sooner or later.' Giancarlo shrugged. 'It happens. Debts accumulate. Shareholders get the jitters. Redundancies have to be made. It's a short step until the liquidators start converging like vultures, and when that happens possessions get seized to pay off disgruntled creditors who are out of pocket.'

Caroline's eyes were like saucers as she imagined this worst-case scenario.

'That would devastate Alberto,' she whispered. She sidled towards the bed and sat down. 'Are you sure about all this? No. Forget I asked that. I forgot that you never make mistakes.'

Giancarlo looked at the forlorn figure on the bed and clicked his tongue impatiently. 'Isn't it a good thing that he'll be spared all of that? No bailiffs showing up at the door, demanding the paintings and the hangings? No bank clamouring for the house to be put on the market to the highest bidder, even if the price is way below its worth?'

'Yes.' She looked at him dubiously.

'So you can wipe that pitiful look from your face immediately!'

'You said that you were going to…what, exactly? Give him the money? Won't that be an awful lot of money? Are you *that* rich?'

'I have enough,' Giancarlo stated drily, amused by her question.

'How much is enough?'

'Enough to ensure that Alberto's house and company don't end up in the hands of the receivers. Of course, there's no such thing as a free lunch.'

'What do you mean?'

'I mean…' He pushed himself away from the window and strolled through the bedroom, taking in all those little signs of neglect that were almost impossible to spot unless you were looking for them. God only knew, the house was ancient. It was probably riddled with all manner of damp, dry rot, termites in the woodwork. Having grown up in a house that dated back centuries, Giancarlo had made sure that his own place was unashamedly modern. Dry rot, damp and termites would never be able to get a foothold.

'I *mean* that what is now my father's will inevitably become mine. I will take over his company and return it to its once-thriving state and naturally I will do the same with this villa. It's in dire need of repair anyway. I'll wager that those rooms that have been closed off will be in the process of falling to pieces.'

'And you won't be doing any of that because you care about Alberto,' Caroline spoke her thoughts aloud while Giancarlo looked at her through narrowed eyes, marvelling at the way every thought running through her head was reflected in the changing nuances of her expressions.

'In fact,' she carried on slowly, her thoughts rearranging themselves in her head to form a complete picture of what was really going on, 'you're not interested in reconciling with your father at all, are you?'

Giancarlo wasn't about to encourage any kind of conversation on what she considered the rights and wrongs of his reasons for coming to the lake, so he maintained a steady silence—although the resigned disappointment in her voice managed to pierce through his rigid self-control in a way that was infuriating. Her huge, accusing eyes were doing the same thing as well and he frowned impatiently.

'It's impossible to reconcile with someone you can barely recall,' he said in a flatly dismissive voice. 'I don't know Alberto.'

'You know him enough to want to hurt him for what you think he did to you.'

'That's a ridiculous assumption!'

'Is it? You said yourself that you were going to buy him out because it would give you the chance to redress injustices.'

Giancarlo was fiercely protective of his private life. He never discussed his past with anyone and many women had tried. They had seen it as a stepping stone to getting to know him better, had mistakenly thought that, with the right amount of encouragement, he would open up and pour his heart out. It was always a fatal flaw.

'Alberto divorced my mother and did everything legally possible to ensure that, whilst the essentials were paid, she was left with the minimum, just enough to get by. From *this*—' he gestured in a sweeping arc to encompass the villa and its fabulous surroundings '—she was reduced to living in a small modern box in the outskirts of Milan. You can see that I carry a certain amount of bitterness towards my father.

'However, it has to be said that, were I a truly vengeful person, I would not have returned here and I certainly would not be contemplating a lucrative buy-out. Lucrative from Alberto's point of view, that is. A lot less lucrative from where I'm standing, because his company will need a great deal of money pouring into it to get it off the starters' gate. Face it, I could have read those financial reports, turned my back, walked away. Waited until I read about the demise of his company in the financial section of the newspapers. Believe me, I seriously considered that option, but then… Let's just say that I opted for the personal touch. So much more satisfying.'

Caroline was finding it impossible to tally up Giancarlo's version of his father with her own experiences of Alberto. Yes, he was undoubtedly difficult and had probably been a thousand times more so when he had been younger, but he wasn't stingy. She just couldn't imagine him being vindictive towards his ex-wife, although how could she know for sure?

One thing she *did* know now was that Giancarlo might justify his actions as redressing a balance but it was revenge of a hands-on variety and no part of her could condone that. He would rescue his father in the certain knowledge that guilt would be Alberto's lifelong companion from then onwards. He would attack Alberto's most vulnerable part: his pride.

She stood up, hands on her hips, and looked at him with blazing eyes.

'I don't care how you put it, that's absolutely *rotten*!'

'*Rotten*, to step in and bail him out?' Giancarlo shook his head grimly and took a couple of steps towards her.

He had his hands in the pockets of his trousers and his movements were leisurely and unhurried, but there was an element of threat in every step he took that brought him closer and Caroline fought to stay her ground. She couldn't wrench her eyes away from him. He had the allure of a dangerous but spectacularly beautiful predator.

Looking down at her, Giancarlo's dark eyes skimmed the hectic flush in her cheeks, her rapid, angry breathing.

'You're a spitfire, aren't you…?' he murmured lazily, which thoroughly disconcerted Caroline. She wasn't used to dealing with men like this. Her experience of the opposite sex was strictly confined to the two men she had dated in the past, both of whom were gentle souls with whom she still shared a comfortable friendship, and work colleagues after she had left school.

'No, I'm not! I never argue. I don't like arguing.'

'You could have fooled me.'

'You do this to me,' she breathed, only belatedly realising that somehow that didn't sound quite right. 'I mean…'

'I get you worked up?'

'Yes! No…'

'Yes? No? Which is it?'

'Stop laughing at me. None of this is funny.' She

drew her cardigan tightly around her in a defensive gesture that wasn't lost on him.

'For a young woman, your choice of clothes is very old-fashioned. Cardigans are for women over forty.'

'I don't see what my clothes have to do with anything.' But she stumbled over her words. Was he trying to throw her? He was succeeding. Now, along with anger was a creeping sense of embarrassment.

'Are you self-conscious about your body?' This was the sort of question Giancarlo never asked any woman. He had never been a big fan of soul-searching conversations. He had always preferred to keep it light, and yet he found that he was really curious about the hell cat who claimed not to be a hell cat. Except when in his presence.

Caroline broke the connection and walked towards the door but she was shaking like a leaf.

She stood in the doorway, half-in, half-out of the bedroom, which suddenly seemed as confining as a prison cell when he was towering above her.

'And when do you intend to tell Alberto everything?'

'I should imagine that he will probably be the

one who brings up the subject,' Giancarlo said, still looking at her, almost regretful that the conversation was back on a level footing. 'You seem to have a lot of faith in human nature. Take it from me, it's misplaced.'

'I don't want you upsetting him. His doctor says that he's to be as stress-free as possible in order to make a full recovery.'

'Okay. Here's the deal. I won't open the conversation with a casual query about the state of his failing company.'

'You really don't care about anyone but yourself, do you?' Caroline asked in a voice tinged with genuine wonder.

'You have a special knack for saying all the wrong things to me,' Giancarlo muttered with a frown.

'What you mean is that I say things you don't want to hear.' She stepped quickly out into the corridor as he walked towards her. She was beginning to understand that being too close to him physically was like standing too close to an electric field. 'We should go downstairs. Alberto will be wondering where we've got to. He tires easily now, so we'll be having an early supper.'

'And tell me, who does the cooking? The same two girls who come in to clean?' He fell into step alongside her, but even though the conversation had moved on to a more neutral topic he was keenly aware of her still clutching the cardigan around her. His first impression had been of someone very background. Now, he was starting to review that initial impression. Underneath the straightforward personality there seemed to be someone very fiery and not easily intimidated. She had taken a deep breath and stood up to him in a way that not very many people did.

'Sometimes. Now that Alberto is on a restricted diet, Tessa tends to prepare his meals, and I cook for myself and Tessa. It's a daily fight to get Alberto to eat bland food. He's fond of saying that there's no life worth living without salt.'

Giancarlo heard the smile in her voice. For his sins, his father had found himself a very devoted companion.

For the first time he wondered what it would have been like to have had Alberto as a father. The man had clearly mellowed over time. Would they have had that connection? How much had he suffered because of his constant warfare with his wife?

Irritated with himself for being drawn back into a past he could not change, Giancarlo focused on sustaining the conversation with a number of innocuous questions as they walked back down the grand staircase, Caroline leading the way towards the smallest of the sitting-rooms at the back of the house.

Even with the majority of the rooms seemingly closed off, there was still a lot of ground to cover. Yet again he found himself wondering what the appeal was for a young woman. Terrific house, great grounds, pleasing views and interesting walks—but take those things out of the equation and boredom would gradually set in, surely?

How bored had his mother been, surrounded by all this ostentatious wealth, trapped like a bird in a gilded cage?

Alberto had met her on one of his many conferences. She had been a sparkling, pretty waitress at the only fancy restaurant in a small town on the Amalfi coast where he had gone to grab a couple of days of rest before the remainder of his business trip. She had been plucked from obscurity and catapulted into wealth, but nothing, she had repeatedly complained to her son over the years following her divorce, could compensate for the horror of living with a man who treated her no better than a servant. She had done her very best, but time and again her efforts had been met with a brick wall. Alberto, she had said with bitterness, had turned out to be little more than a difficult, unyielding and unforgiving man, years too old for her, who had thwarted all her attempts at having fun.

Giancarlo had been conditioned to loathe the man whom his mother had held responsible for all her misfortunes.

Except now he was prey to a disturbing sensation of doubt as he heard Caroline chatter on about his father. How disagreeable could the man be if she was so attached to him? Was it possible for a leopard to change its spots to that extreme extent?

Before they reached the sitting-room, she paused to rest one small hand lightly on his arm.

'Do you promise that you won't upset him?'

'I'm not big into making promises.'

'Why is it so hard to get through to you?'

'Believe it or not, most people don't have a problem. In our case, we might just as well be from different planets, occupying different time zones. I told you I won't greet him with an enquiry about the health of his finances, and I won't. Beyond that, I promise nothing.'

'Just try to get to know him,' Caroline pleaded, her huge brown eyes welded to his as she dithered with her hand still on his arm. 'I just can't believe you know the real Alberto.'

Giancarlo's mouth thinned and he stared down pointedly at her hand before looking down at her, his dark eyes as cold and frozen as the lake in winter.

'Don't presume to tell me what I know or don't know,' he said with ice in his voice, and Caroline removed her hand quickly as though she had been burnt suddenly. 'I've come here for a purpose and, whether you like it or not, I will ensure that things are wrapped up before I leave.'

'And how long are you intending to stay? I never asked, but you really haven't come with very much luggage, have you? I mean, one small bag…'

'Put it this way, there will be no need to go shopping for food on my account. I plan on being here no longer than two days. Three at the very most.'

Caroline's heart sank further. This was a business visit, however you dressed it up and tried to call it something else. Two days? Just long enough for Giancarlo to levy his charge for Alberto's past wrongdoings, whatever those might have been, with interest.

She didn't think that he was even prepared to get to know his father. The only thing that interested him, his only motivation for coming to the villa, was to dole out his version of revenge, whether he chose to call it that or not.

'Now, any more questions?' Giancarlo drawled and Caroline shook her head miserably, not trusting herself to speak. Once again, he felt a twinge of uninvited and unwelcome doubt. 'I'm surprised at your level of attachment to Alberto,' he commented brusquely, annoyed at himself, because would her answer change anything? No.

'Why?' Her eyes were wide and clear when she looked at him. 'I didn't have a load of prejudices when I came here. I came with an open mind. I found a lonely old man with a kind heart and a generous nature. Yes, he might be prickly, but it's what's inside that counts. At least, that's how it works for me.'

He really shouldn't have been diverted into encouraging her opinion. He should have known that whatever chirpy, homespun answer she came out with would get on his nerves. He was very tempted to inform her that he was the least prejudiced person on the face of the earth, that if on this single occasion he was prey to a very natural inclination towards one or two preconceived ideas about Alberto, then no one could lay the blame for that at his door. He cut short the infuriating desire to be sidetracked.

'Well, I'm very pleased that he has you around,' Giancarlo said neutrally. Caroline bristled because she could just *sense* that he was being patronising.

'No, you aren't. You're still so mad at him that you probably would much rather have preferred it if he was still on his own in this big, rambling house with no one to talk to. And, if there *was* someone around, then I'm sure you'd rather it wasn't me, because you don't like me at all!'

'What gives you that idea?'

Caroline ignored that question. The promise of what was to come felt like a hangman's noose around her neck. She was fit to explode. 'Well, I don't like you either,' she declared with vehemence. 'And I hope you choke on your plans to ruin Alberto's life.' She spun away from him so that he couldn't witness the tears stinging her eyes. 'He's waiting for you,' she muttered in a driven voice. 'Why don't you go in now and get it over with?'

CHAPTER FOUR

GIANCARLO entered a room that was familiar to him. The smallest of the sitting-rooms at the back of the house had always been the least ornate and hence the cosiest. Out of nowhere came the memory of doing his homework in this very room, always resisting the urge to sneak outside, down to the lake. French doors led out to the sprawling garden that descended to the lake via a series of landscaped staircases. Alberto sat in a chair by one of the bay windows with a plaid rug over his legs even though it was warm in the room.

'So, my boy, you've come.'

Giancarlo looked at his father with a shuttered expression. He wondered if his memory was playing tricks on him, because Alberto looked diminished. In his head, he realised that he had held on to a memory that was nearly two decades old and clearly out of date.

'Father...'

'Caroline. You're gaping. Why don't you offer a drink to our guest? And I will have a whisky while you're about it.'

'You'll have no such thing.' Back on familiar ground, Caroline moved past Giancarlo to adopt a protective stance by her employer, who made feeble attempts to flap her away. Looking at their interaction, Giancarlo could see that it was a game with which they were both comfortable and familiar.

Just for a few seconds, he was the outsider looking in, then that peculiar feeling was gone as the tableau shifted. Caroline walked across to a cupboard which had been reconfigured to house a small fridge, various snacks and cartons of juice.

He was aware of her chattering nervously, something about it being time efficient to have stuff at hand for Alberto because this was his favourite room in the house and he just wasn't as yet strong enough to continually make long trips to the kitchen if he needed something to drink.

'Of course, it's all supervised,' she babbled away, while the tension stretched silent and invisible in the room. 'No whisky here. Tessa and I know that that's Alberto's Achilles' heel so we have wine. I put some in earlier, would that be okay?' She kept her eyes firmly averted from the uncomfortable sight of father and son, but in her head she was picturing them circling one another, making their individual, quiet assessments.

Given half a chance, she would have run for cover to another part of the house, but her instinct to protect Alberto kept her rooted to the spot.

When she finally turned around, with drinks and snacks on a little tray, it was to find that Giancarlo had taken up position on one of the chairs. If he was in any way uncomfortable, he wasn't showing it.

'Well, Father, I have been told that you've suffered a heart attack—'

'How was the drive here, Giancarlo? Still too many cars in the villages?'

They both broke into speech at the same time. Caroline drank too much far too quickly to calm her nerves and lapsed into an awkward silence as ultra-polite questions were fielded with ultra-polite answers. She wondered if they were aware that many of their mannerisms were identical— the way they both shifted and leaned forward when a remark was made; the way they idly held their glasses, slightly stroking the rim with their fingers. They should have bonded without question. Instead, Giancarlo's cool, courteous conversation was the equivalent of a door being shut.

He was here. He was talking. But he was not conversing.

At least he had kept his word and nothing, so far, had been mentioned about the state of Alberto's finances, although she knew that her employer must surely be curious to know why his son had bothered to make the trip out to Lake Como when he displayed so little enthusiasm for the end result.

Dinner was a light soup, followed by fish. One of the local girls had been brought in, along with the two regular housekeepers, to take care of the cooking and the clearing away. So, instead of eating in the kitchen, they dined in the formal dining-room, which proved to be a mistake.

The long table and the austere surroundings were not conducive to light-hearted conversation. Tessa had volunteered to have her meal in the small sitting-room adjoining her bedroom, in order to give them all some space to chat without her hovering over Alberto, checking to make sure he stuck to his diet. Caroline heartily wished she could have joined her, because the atmosphere was thick with tension.

By the time they had finished their starters and made adequately polite noises about it, several topics of conversation had been started and quickly abandoned. The changes in the weather patterns had been discussed, as had the number of tourists at the lakes, the lack of snow the previous winter and, of course, Alberto asked Giancarlo about his work, to which he received such brief replies that that too was a subject quickly shelved.

By the time the main course was brought to them—and Alberto had bemoaned the fact that they were to dine on fish rather than something altogether heartier like a slab of red meat—Caroline had frankly had enough of the painfully stilted conversation.

If they didn't want to have any kind of meaningful conversation together, then she would fill in the gaps. She talked about her childhood, growing up in Devon. Her parents were both teachers, very much into being 'green'. She laughed at memories of the chickens they had kept that laid so many eggs at times that her mother would bake cakes a family of three had no possibility of eating just to get rid of some of them. She would contribute them to the church every Sunday and one year was actually awarded a special prize for her efforts.

She talked about exchange students, some of whom had been most peculiar, and joked about her mother's experiments in the kitchen with home-grown produce from their small garden. In the end, she and her father had staged a low-level rebellion until normal food was reintroduced. Alberto chuckled but he was not relaxed. It was there in the nervous flickering of his eyes and his subdued, downturned mouth. The son he had desperately wanted to see didn't want to see him and he wasn't even bothering to try to hide the fact.

All the while she could feel Giancarlo's dark eyes restively looking at her and she found that she just couldn't look at him. What was it about him that brought her out in goose bumps and made her feel as though she just wasn't comfortable in her own skin? The timbre of his low, husky voice sent shivers down her spine, and when he turned to look at her she was aware of her body in such miniscule detail that she burned with discomfort.

By the time they adjourned for coffee back in the small sitting-room, Caroline was exhausted and she could see that Alberto was flagging. Giancarlo, on the other hand, was as coldly composed as he had been at the start of the evening.

'How long do you plan on staying, my boy? You should get yourself out on the lake. Beautiful weather. And you were always fond of your sailing. Of course, we no longer have the sailboat. What was the point? After, well, after…'

'After what, Father?'

'I think it's time you went to bed, Alberto,' Caroline interjected desperately as the conversation finally threatened to explode. 'You're flagging and you know the doctor said that you really need to take it easy. I'll get hold of Tessa and—'

'After you and your mother left.'

'Ah, so finally you've decided to acknowledge that you ever had a wife. One could be forgiven for thinking that you had erased her from your memory completely.' No mention had been made of Adriana. Not one single word. They had tiptoed around all mention of the past, as though it had never existed. Alberto had been on his best behaviour. Now Giancarlo expected to see his real father, the cold, unforgiving one, the one who, from memory, had never shied away from arguing.

'I've done no such thing, my son,' Alberto surprised Giancarlo by saying quietly.

'It's time you went to bed, Alberto.' Caroline stood up and looked pointedly at Giancarlo. 'I will not allow you to tire your father out any longer,' she said, and in truth Alberto was showing signs of strain around his eyes. 'He's been very ill and this conversation is *not* going to help anything at all.'

'Oh, do stop fussing, Caroline.' But his pocket handkerchief was in his hand and he was patting his forehead wearily.

'*You*—' she jabbed a finger at Giancarlo '—are going to wait *right here* for me while I go to fetch Tessa because I intend to have a little chat with you.'

'The boy wants to talk about his past, Caroline. It's why he's come.'

Caroline snorted without taking her eyes away from Giancarlo's beautiful face. If only Alberto knew!

She spun back around to look at her employer. 'I'm going to fetch Tessa and tomorrow you won't have your routine disrupted. Your son is going to be here for a few days. There will be time enough to take a trip down memory lane.'

'A few days?' They both said the same thing at the same time. Giancarlo was appalled and enraged while Alberto was hesitantly hopeful. Caroline decided to favour Giancarlo with a confirming nod.

'Maybe even as long as a week,' she threw at him, because wasn't it better to be hanged for a sheep than a lamb? 'I believe that's what you said to me?' She wondered where on earth this fierce determination was coming from. She always shied away from confrontation!

'So tomorrow,' she continued to both men, 'there will be no need for you to worry about entertaining your son, Alberto. He will be sailing on the lake.'

'I'll be *sailing on the lake*?'

'Correct. With me.' This in case he decided to argue the rules she was confidently laying down, with a silent prayer in her head that he wasn't going to launch into an outraged argument which would devastate Alberto, especially after the gruesome evening they had just spent together.

'I thought you couldn't sail, Caroline,' Alberto murmured and she drew herself up to her unimpressive height of a little over five-three.

'But I've been counting down the days I could start learning.'

'You told me that you had a morbid fear of open water.'

'It's something I've been told I can only overcome by facing it…on open water. It's a well-known fact that, er, that you have to confront your fears to overcome them…'

She backed out of the room before Alberto could pin her down and flew to Tessa's room. She could picture the awkward conversation taking place between Giancarlo and Alberto in her absence, and that was a best-case scenario. The worst-case scenario involved them both taking that trip down memory lane, the one she had temporarily managed to divert. It was a trip that could only lead to the sort of heated argument that would do no good to Alberto's fragile recovery. With that in mind, she ran back to the sitting-room like a bat out of hell and was breathless by the time she reappeared ten minutes later.

It was to discover that Giancarlo had disappeared.

'The boy has work to do,' Alberto told her.

'At this hour?'

'I remember when I was a young man, I used to work all the hours God made. Boy's built like me, which might not be such a good thing. Hard work is fine but the important thing is to know when to stop. He's a fine-looking lad, don't you think?'

'I suppose there might be some who like that sort of look,' Caroline said dismissively. With relief, she heard Tessa approaching. Alberto drew no limits when it came to asking whatever difficult questions he had in his head. It was, he had proclaimed, one of the benefits of being an old bore. The last thing she wanted was to have an in-depth question-and-answer session on what she thought of his son.

'Bright, too.'

Caroline wondered how he could be so clearly generous in his praise for someone who had made scant effort to meet him halfway. She made an inarticulate noise under her breath and tried not to scowl.

'Said he'd meet you by his car at nine tomorrow morning,' Alberto told her, while simultaneously trying to convince Tessa, who had entered the room at a brisk pace, that he didn't need to be treated like a child all the time. 'Think he'll enjoy a spot of sailing. It'll relax him. He seems tense. Of course, I totally understand that, given the circumstances. So don't you mind me, my dear. Think I'll rise and shine, but not with the larks, and the old bat here can take me for my constitutional walk.'

Tessa winked at Caroline and grinned behind Alberto's back as she helped him up.

'Anyone would think he wasn't a complete poppet when I settle him at night,' she said, unfazed.

Having issued her dictate to Giancarlo for 'a chat', Caroline realised that chatting was the last thing she wanted to do with him. All her bravado had seeped out of her. The prospect of a morning in his company now seemed like an uphill climb. Would he listen to her? He hadn't as yet revealed to Alberto the real reason for his visit but he would the following day; she knew it. Just as he would declare that his visit was not going to last beyond forty-eight hours, despite what she had optimistically announced to Alberto.

There was no way that she would be able to persuade Giancarlo into doing anything he didn't want to do and the past few hours had shown her that grasping the olive branch was definitely not on his agenda.

She had a restless night. The villa was beautiful but no modernisation had taken place for a very long time. Air-conditioning was unheard of and the air was still and sluggish.

She barely felt rested when she opened her eyes the following morning at eight-thirty. It took her a few seconds to remember that her normal routine was out of sync. She wouldn't be having a leisurely breakfast with Alberto before taking him for a walk, then after lunch settling into sifting through some of his first-edition books which, in addition to his memoirs, was one of her jobs for him: sorting them into order so that he could decide which ones might be left to the local museum and which would be kept. He had all manner of historical information about the district, a great deal of which was contained in the various letters and journals of his ancestors. It was a laborious but enjoyable task which she would be missing in favour of a sailing trip with Giancarlo.

She dressed quickly: a pair of trousers, a striped tee shirt and, of course, her cardigan, a blue one this time; covered shoes. She didn't know anything at all about being on a boat, but she knew enough to suspect that a skirt and sandals would not be the required get-up. Impatiently, she tied her hair back in a long braid for the purpose of practicality.

There was no time for breakfast and she walked from one wing of the villa to the other, emerging outside into a blissfully sunny day with cloudless skies, bright turquoise shot through with milk. Giancarlo was standing by his car, sunglasses on, talking into his mobile phone. For a few seconds she stared at him, her heart thudding. He might have severed all ties with his aristocratic background, but he couldn't erase it from the contours of his face. Even in tattered clothes and barefoot he would still look the ultimate sophisticate.

He glanced across, registered her presence and snapped shut his phone to lounge indolently against the car as she walked towards him.

'So,' he drawled, staring down at her when she

was finally in front of him. 'I'm apparently here on a one-week vacation.' He removed the sunglasses to dangle them idly between his fingers while he continued to look at her until she felt herself blush to the roots of her hair.

'Yes, well…'

'Maybe you could tell me how I had this week planned out? Bearing in mind that you seemed to have arranged it.'

'You *could* make just a little polite conversation before you start laying into me.'

'Was I doing that?' He pushed himself off the car and swung round to open the door for her, slamming it shut as she clambered into the passenger seat. 'I distinctly recall having told you that the most I would be staying would be a matter of two days. Tell me how you saw fit to extend that into a week?' He had bent down, propping himself against the car with both hands so that he could question her through her open window. He felt so close up and personal that she found herself taking deep breaths and gasping for air.

'Yes, I realise that,' Caroline muttered mutinously when he showed no signs of backing off. 'But you made me mad.'

'I—made—you—mad?'

Caroline nodded mutely and stared straight ahead, keenly aware of his hawk-like eyes boring into her averted profile. She visibly sagged when he strode round to get into the car.

'And how,' he asked softly, 'do you think I felt when you backed me into a corner?'

'Yes, well, you deserved it!'

'Do you know, I can't believe you.' He exited the gravelled courtyard with a screeching of angry tyres and she clenched her fists so tightly that she could feel her nails biting into the palms of her hands. 'I didn't come here for relaxation!'

'I know! Don't you think you made that pretty obvious last night?'

'I gave you my word that I wouldn't introduce the contentious issue of money on day one. I kept my word.'

'*Just about.* You didn't make the slightest effort with Alberto. You just sat there *sneering*, and okay, so maybe I was wrong to imply that you were staying a tiny bit longer than you had planned.'

'You are the master of understatement!'

'But when you mentioned your mother, well, I

just wanted to avert an argument, so possibly I said the first thing that came into my head. Look, I'm sorry. I guess you could always tell Alberto that I made a mistake, that I got the dates wrong. I know you have lots of important things to do and probably can't spare a week off, whatever the reason, but just then I didn't think I had a choice. I had to take the sting out of the evening, give Alberto something to hang on to.'

'What a shame you couldn't use your brain and think things through before you jumped in feet first! I take it the little *chat* you had in mind last night has now been covered?'

'It was an awkward evening. Alberto really tried to make conversation. Do you know, after you disappeared to work he actually seemed to understand? It was almost as though he wasn't prepared to see anything wrong in his son coming to see him for the first time in years, barely making an effort and then vanishing to work!'

Giancarlo flushed darkly. The evening had not gone quite as he had envisaged, and now he wasn't entirely sure *what* he had envisaged. He just knew that the argumentative man—the one who had loomed larger than life in his head thanks to Adriana's continuing bitterness; the one who would have made it so easy for him to treat with the patronising contempt he had always assumed would be richly deserved—had not lived up to expectations.

For starters, it was clear that Alberto's ill health was every bit as grave as Caroline had stated, and even more surprising, instead of a conversation spiked with the sort of malice and bitterness to which he had become accustomed with his mother over the years, there had been no mention made of a regrettable past and a miserable marriage. Alberto had been so wildly different from the picture in his head that Giancarlo had spent the time when he should have been working trying to figure out the discrepancies.

Naturally, the question of money, the *raison d'être* for his presence at the villa, would rear its ugly head in due course. He might have been weirdly taken aback at the man he had found, but sooner or later the inevitable begging bowl would emerge. However, not even that certainty could still the uneasy doubt that had crept stealthily through him after he had vacated the sitting-room.

'Perhaps,' he said, glancing around at scenery that felt more familiar with every passing second, 'a few days away from Milan might not be such a terrible idea.' The very second he said it, Giancarlo knew that he had made the right decision.

'Sorry?'

'I wouldn't call it a holiday, but it is certainly more restful here than it is in Milan.' He looked sideways at Caroline. Through the open window, the breeze was wreaking havoc with her attempts at a neat, sensible hair-style, flinging it into disarray.

'I guess you don't really do holidays,' she said tentatively. Even if his intention was still to consume his father's house and company, a few days spent with Alberto might render him a little less black and white in his judgement, might invest him with sufficient tact so that Alberto wasn't humiliated.

'Time is money.'

'There's more to life than money.'

'Agreed. Unfortunately, it usually takes money to enjoy those things.'

'Why have you decided to stay on? Just a short

while ago you were really angry that I had put you in a difficult position.'

'But put me in it you did, and I'm a man who thinks on his feet and adjusts to situations. So I might be here for a bit longer than I had anticipated. It could only work to my advantage when it comes to constructing the sort of business proposal my father will understand. I'll confess that Alberto isn't the man I had expected. I initially thought that talk of his ill health might have been exaggerated.'

His eyes slid across to her face. Predictably, her expression was one of tight-lipped anger. 'Now I see for myself that he is not a well man, which would no doubt explain his unnaturally docile manner. I am not a monster. I had intended to confront him with his financial predicament without bothering with the tedious process of beating around the bush. Now I accept that I might have to tiptoe towards the conclusion I want.'

The scenery rushing past him, the feeling of open space and translucent light, was breathtaking. He was behind the wheel of a car, he was driving through clear open spaces with a view of glittering blue water ahead, and for the first time in years he felt light-headed with a rushing sense of freedom.

'Besides,' he mused lazily, 'I haven't been to this part of the world for a long time.'

He was following signs to one of the many sailing jetties scattered around the lake and now he swerved off the main road, heading down towards the glittering water.

Caroline forgot all her misgivings about Giancarlo's mission. She forgot how angry and upset she was at the thought of Alberto being on the receiving end of a son who had only agreed to see him out of a misplaced desire for revenge.

'I don't think I can go through with this,' she muttered as the car slowed to a stop.

Giancarlo killed the engine and turned to face her. 'Wasn't this whole sailing trip *your* idea?'

'It was supposed to be *your* sailing trip.' There were tourists milling around and the sailing boats bobbed like colourful playthings on the calm water. Out on the lake many more of them skirted over the aquamarine surface. At any given moment, one might very well sink, and where would that leave those happy, smiling tourists on board? She blanched and licked her lips nervously.

'You're white as a sheet.'

'Yes, well…'

'You're seriously scared of water?'

'Of *open* water. Anything could happen. Especially on something as flimsy as a sailboat.'

'Anything could happen to anyone, anywhere. Driving here was probably more of a risk than that boat out there.' He opened his door and swung his long body out, moving round to open the passenger door for her. 'You were right when you said that you can't kill an irrational fear unless you confront it.' He held out one hand and, heart beating fast, Caroline took it. The feel of his fingers as they curled around hers was warm and comforting.

'How would you know?' she asked in a shaky voice as she eased herself out of the car and half-eyed the lake the way a minnow might eye a patch of shark-infested water. 'I bet you've never been scared of anything in your life.'

'I'll take that as a compliment.' He kept his fingers interlinked with hers as he led her down towards the jetty.

Hell, he never thought he'd live to see the day when there were no thoughts of work, deals to be done or lawyers to meet impinging on his mind. His mother's uncertain finances—the details of which he had never been spared, even when he had been too young to fully understand them—had bred a man to whom the acquisition of money was akin to a primal urge. The fact that he was very, very good at it had only served to strengthen his rampant ambition. Women had come and gone, and would continue to come and go, for his parents were a sad indictment of the institution of marriage, but the challenge of work would always be a constant.

Except, now, it appeared to have taken a back seat.

And he barely recognised the boyish feeling inside him as her fingers tightly squeezed his the closer they got to the jetty.

'Hey, trust me,' he told her. 'It'll be worth it. There's nothing like the freedom of being out on the lake and it's not like being on the sea. The edge of the lake is always visible. You'll always be able to orienteer yourself by the horizon.'

'How deep is it?'

'Don't think about that. Tell me why you're so scared.'

Caroline hesitated. She disapproved of everything about this man and yet his invitation to confide was irresistible. *And* her fingers were still entwined with his. Suddenly conscious of that, she wriggled them, which encouraged him to grasp them slightly harder.

'Well?'

'I fell in a river when I was a child.' She sighed and glanced up at him sheepishly. 'I must have been about seven, just learning how to swim. There were four of us and it was the summer holidays. Our parents had all arranged this picnic in the woods.'

'Sounds idyllic.'

'It was, until the four of us kids went off to do a bit of exploring. We were crossing a bridge, just messing around. Looking back now, the river must not have been more than a metre deep and the bridge was just a low, rickety thing. We were playing that game, the one where you send a twig from one side of the bridge and race to the other side to see it float out. Anyway, I fell, headlong into the river. It was terrifying. Although I could swim enough to get out, it was as though my mind had blanked that out. All I could taste was the water and I could feel floating weeds on my face. I thought I was going to drown. Everyone was screaming. The adults were with us within seconds and there was no harm done, but ever since then I've hated the thought of open water.'

'And when I was fourteen, I tried my hand at horse riding and came off at the first hurdle. Ever since then I've had an irrational fear of horses.'

'No, you haven't.' But she grinned up at him, shading her eyes from the glare of the sun with one hand.

'You're right. I haven't. But it's a possibility. I've never been near a horse in my life. I can ski down any black run but I suspect a horse would have me crying with terror.'

Caroline laughed. She was relaxing, barely noticing that the sailboat was being rented, because Giancarlo had continued to talk to her in the soothing voice of someone intent on calming a skittish animal, describing silly scenarios that made her smile. He was certain that he would have a fear of horses. Spiders brought him out in a sweat. Birds brought to mind certain horror movies. He knew that he would definitely have had a phobia of small aircraft had he not managed to successfully bypass that by owning his own helicopter.

Giancarlo hadn't put this much effort into a woman in a long time. It was baffling, because had someone told him a week ago that he would be held to account by a woman who didn't know the meaning of tact, he would have laughed out loud. And had that someone then said that he would find himself holed up at his father's villa for a week, courtesy of the same woman who didn't know the meaning of tact, he would have called out the little men with strait-jackets because the idea was beyond ridiculous.

Yet here he was: reaching out to help a woman with unruly brown hair streaked with caramel, who didn't seem to give a damn about all the other nonsense other women cared about, onto a sailboat. And enjoying the fact that he had managed to distract her from her fear of water by making her laugh.

Obeying an instinctive need to rationalise his actions, Giancarlo easily justified his uncharacteristic behaviour by assuming that this was simply his creative way of dealing with a situation. So what would have been the point in tearing her off a strip for having coerced him into staying at the villa longer than he had planned? He would still do what he had come to do, and anyway it made a relaxing change to interact with a woman in whom he had no sexual interest. He went for tall, thin blondes with a penchant for high-end designer clothes. So take away the sometimes-tedious game of chase and catch with a woman and it seemed that he was left with something really quite enjoyable.

Caroline was on the sailboat before she really realised what had happened. One minute she was laughing, enjoying his silly remarks with the sun on her face and the breeze running its balmy fingers through her hair and gradually undoing her loose plait—the next minute, terra firma was no longer beneath her feet and the swaying of the boat was forcibly reminding her of everything she feared about being out at sea, or in this case out on the lake.

Did he even know how to handle this thing? Wasn't he supposed to have had a little pep talk from the guys in charge of the rentals—a refresher course in how to make sure this insignificant piece of plywood with a bit of cloth didn't blow over when they were in the middle of the lake?

Giancarlo saw her stricken face, the panicked way she looked over her shoulder at the safety of a shoreline from which they were drifting.

He reacted on pure gut impulse.

He kissed her. He curled his long fingers into her tangle of dark hair and with one hand pulled her towards him. The taste of her full lips was like nectar. He felt her soft, lush body curve into him, felt her full breasts squash softly against his chest. He had taken her utterly by surprise and there was no resistance as the kiss grew deeper and more intimately exploring, tasting every part of her sweet mouth. God, he wanted to do more! His arousal was fast and hard and his fabled self-control disappeared so quickly that he was at the mercy of his senses for the first time in his life.

He wanted to strip off her shirt, tear off her bra, which wouldn't be one of those lacy slips of nothing the women he dated wore but something plainly, resolutely and impossibly sexy. He wanted to lose himself in her generous breasts until he stopped thinking altogether.

Caroline was in the grip of something so intensely powerful that she could barely breathe.

She had never felt like this in her life before. She could feel her body melting, could feel her nipples tightening and straining against her bra, knew that she was hot and wet between her legs…

Her body was behaving in a way it had never behaved before and it thrilled and terrified her at the same time.

When he eventually broke free, she literally felt lost.

'You kissed me,' she breathed, still clutching him by the shirt and looking up at him with huge, searching eyes. She wanted to know *why*. She knew why *she* had responded! Underneath her disapproval for everything he had done and said, there was a strong, irresistible current of pure physical attraction. She had been swept along by it and nothing she had ever experienced in her life before had prepared her for its ferocity. Lust was just something she had read about. Now she knew, firsthand, how powerful it could be. Was he feeling the same thing? Did he want to carry on kissing her as much as she wanted him to?

She gradually became aware of their surroundings and of the fact that, with one hand, he had expertly guided the small sailboat away from shore and out into the open lake. They had become one of the small bright toys she had glimpsed from land.

'You kissed me. Was that to distract me from the fact that we were heading away from land?'

Hell, how did *he* know? He just knew that he had been blown away, had lost all shreds of self-control. It was not something of which he was proud, nor could he understand it. Rallying quickly, he recovered his shattered equilibrium and took a couple of steps back, but then had to look away briefly because her flushed cheeks and parted mouth were continuing to play havoc with his libido.

'It worked, didn't it?' He nodded towards the shore, still not trusting himself to look at her properly. 'You're on the water now and, face it, you're no longer scared.'

CHAPTER FIVE

CAROLINE remained positioned in the centre of
the small boat for the next hour. She made sure
not to look out to the water, which made her instantly conjure up drowning scenarios in her head.
Instead, she looked at Giancarlo. It was blissfully
easy to devote all her attention to him. He might
not have sailed for a long time but whatever he
had learnt as a boy had returned to him with ease.

'It's like riding a bike,' he explained, doing
something clever with the rudder. 'Once learnt,
never forgotten.'

Caroline found herself staring at his muscular brown legs, sprinkled with dark hair. Having
brought just enough clothes to cover a one-night
stay, he had, he had admitted when asked, pulled
strings and arranged for one of the local shops to
open up early for him. At eight that morning, he
had taken his car to the nearest small town and
bought himself a collection of everyday wear. The

khaki shorts and loose-fitting shirt, virtually unbuttoned all the way down, were part of that ward-
robe and they offered her an incredible view of
his highly toned body. Every time he moved, she
could see the ripple of his muscles.

Now he was explaining to her how he had managed to acquire his expertise in a boat. He had
always been drawn to the water. He had had his
first sailing lesson at the age of five and by the
age of ten had been adept enough to sail on his
own, although he had not been allowed. By the
time he had left the lake for good, he could have
crewed his own sailboat, had he been of legal age.

Caroline nodded, murmured and thought about
that kiss. She had been kissed before but never
like that. Neither of the two boyfriends she'd had
had ever made her feel as though the ground was
spinning and freewheeling under her feet; neither
had ever made her feel as if the rules of time and
space had altered, throwing her into a wildly different dimension. With an eye for detail she never
knew she possessed, she marvelled at how a face
so coldly, exquisitely beautiful could inspire such
craven weakness deep inside her when she had
never previously been drawn to men because of

how they looked. She wondered at the way she had fallen headlong into that kiss, never wanting it to stop when she barely liked the guy she had been kissing.

'Hello? Calling Planet Earth…'

'Huh?' Caroline blinked and realised that the sailboat was now practically at a standstill. The sound of the water lapping gently against the sides was mesmeric.

'If you stay in that position any longer, your joints will seize up,' Giancarlo informed her drily. 'Stand up. Walk about.'

'What if I topple the boat over and fall in?'

'Then I'll rescue you. But you'll be easier to rescue if you stripped off to your swimsuit. You *are* wearing a swimsuit underneath those clothes, aren't you?'

'Of course I am!'

'Then, off you go.' To show the way, he dispensed with his shirt, which was damp from his exertions, and laid it flat to dry.

Caroline felt her breath catch painfully in her throat as all her misbehaving senses went into immediate overdrive. Her lips felt swollen and her breasts were tender. She wanted to tell him to look away but knew that that would have been childish. She gave herself a stern little lecture—how many times had she worn this swimsuit? Hundreds! In summer, she would often go down to the beach with her friends. She never went in the water but she lazed and tanned and had never, not once, felt remotely self-conscious.

With a mental shrug, she quickly peeled off her clothes, folding them neatly and accepting the soft towel which Giancarlo had packed in a water-proof bag, then she stood up and took a few tentative steps towards the side of the boat. In truth, she felt much, much calmer than when she had first stepped on the small vessel. There were far too many other things on her mind to focus on her fears.

Watching her, Giancarlo felt a sudden, unexpected rush of pure sexual awareness. She was staring out to sea, her profile to him, offering him a view of the most voluptuous body he had ever laid eyes on, even though her one-piece black swimsuit was the last word in old-fashioned and strove to conceal as much as possible. She had the perfect hourglass figure that would drive most men mad. With the breeze making a nonsense of her plait, she had finally unravelled it and her hair fell in curls almost to her waist. He found that his breathing had become shallow, and his arousal was so prominent and painful that he inhaled sharply and began busying himself with the other towel which he had packed.

A youth spent on water had primed him for certain necessities: towels, drinks, something to snack on and, of course, sun-tan lotion.

He had taken up a safer position, sitting on his towel, when she turned to him with a little frown. He was tempted to tell her to cover herself up as he looked through half-closed eyes at her luscious breasts, which not even her sensible swimsuit could downplay.

'I never even asked,' Caroline said abruptly. 'Are you married?' Proud of herself for having ventured into the unknown and terrifying realms of standing at the side of the boat, she now made her way to where he was sitting and spread her towel alongside his to sit.

'Do I look like a married man?'

Caroline considered her father. 'No,' she admitted. 'And I know that you're not wearing a wedding ring, but lots of married men don't like jewellery of any kind. My dad doesn't.'

'Not married. No intention of ever getting married. You're staring at me as though I've just announced a ban on Christmas Day. Have I shocked you?'

'I just don't understand how you can be so certain of something.'

Giancarlo remained silent for such a long time that she wondered whether he was going to answer. He was now lying down on the towel, his hands folded behind his head, a brooding, dangerous Adonis in repose.

'I don't talk about my private life.'

'I'm not asking you to bare your soul. I was just curious.' She hitched her legs up and wrapped her arms around them. 'You're so… uptight.'

'Me—*uptight*?' Giancarlo looked at her with incredulity.

'It's as though you're scared of ever really letting go.'

'Scared? *Uptight?*'

'I don't mean to be offensive.'

'I never knew I had such a boundless capacity

for patience,' Giancarlo confessed in a staggered voice. 'Do you ever think before you speak?'

'I wouldn't have said those things if you had just answered my question but it doesn't matter now.'

Giancarlo sighed heavily and raked his fingers through his hair in sheer frustration as Caroline stubbornly lay down, closed her eyes and enjoyed the sunshine.

'I've seen firsthand how unreliable the institution of marriage is,' he admitted gruffly. 'And I'm not just talking about the wonderful example set by my parents. The statistics prove conclusively that only an idiot would fall for that fairy-tale nonsense.'

Caroline opened her eyes, propped herself up on one elbow and looked at him with disbelief.

'I'm one of those so-called idiots.'

'Now, I wonder why I'm not entirely surprised?'

'What right do you have to say that?'

Giancarlo held both hands up in surrender. 'I don't want to get into an argument with you, Caroline. The weather's glorious, I haven't been out on a sailboat for the longest while. In fact, this is pretty much the first unscheduled vacation I've had in years. I don't want to spoil it.' He waited for a few seconds and then raised his eyebrows with amusement. 'You mean you aren't going to argue with me?' He shot her a crooked grin that made her go bright red.

'I hate arguing.'

'You could have fooled me.'

But he was still grinning lazily at her. She felt all hot and flustered just looking at him, although she couldn't drag her eyes away. It was impossibly still out here, with just the sound of gentle water and the far-away laughter of people on the nearest sailboat, which was still a good distance away. Suddenly, and for no reason, Caroline felt as though they were a million miles from civilisation, caged in their own intensely private moment. Right now, she wanted nothing more than to be kissed by him again, and that decadent yearning was so shocking that her mouth fell half-open and she found that she was holding her breath.

'Okay, but you have to admit that you give me lots to argue about.'

'I absolutely have to admit that, do I?'

The soft, teasing amusement in his voice made her blush even harder. Suddenly it seemed very important that she remind herself of all the various reasons she had for disliking Giancarlo. She loathed arguing and had never been very good at it, but right now arguing seemed the safest solution to the slow, burning, treacly feeling threatening to send her mind and body off on some weird, scary tangent.

'So, what about girlfriends?' she threw recklessly at him.

'What about *girlfriends*?' Giancarlo couldn't quite believe that she was continuing a conversation which he had deemed to be already closed. She had propped herself up on one elbow so that she was now lying on her side, like a figure from some kind of crazily erotic masterpiece. The most tantalizing thing about her was that he was absolutely convinced that she had no idea of her sensational pulling power.

'Well, I mean, is there someone special in your life at the moment?'

'Why do you ask?'

'I… I just don't want to talk about Alberto…' Caroline clutched at that explanation. In truth, the murky business between Giancarlo and his father seemed a very distant problem as they bobbed on the sailboat, surrounded by the azure blue of the placid lake.

'And nosing where you don't belong is the next best thing?' He should have been outraged at the cavalier way with which she was overstepping his boundaries, but he didn't appear to be. He shrugged. 'No. There's no one special in my life, as you call it, at the moment. The last special woman in my life was two months ago.'

'What was she like?'

'Compliant and undemanding for the first two months. Less so until I called it a day two months later. It happens.'

'I guess most women want more than just a casual fling. Most women like to imagine that things are going to go somewhere after a while.'

'I know. It's a critical mistake.' Giancarlo never made it a habit to enquire about women's pasts. The present was all that interested him. The past was another country, the future a place in which the less interest shown, the better.

Breaking all his own self-imposed restrictions, he asked, with idle curiosity, 'And what about you? Now that we've decided to shelve our arguments over Alberto for a while, you never told me how it is that someone of your age could be tempted to while away an indefinite amount of time in the middle of nowhere with only an old man for company. And forget all that nonsense about enjoying walks in the garden and burying yourself in old books. Did you come to Italy because you were running away from something?'

'Running away from what?' Caroline asked in genuine bewilderment.

'Who knows? Maybe the country idyll proved too much, maybe you got involved with someone who didn't quite fit the image, was that it? Was there some guy lurking in paradise who broke your heart? Was that why you escaped to Italy? Why you're content to hide away in a big, decaying villa? Makes sense. Only child…lots of expectations there…doting parents. Did you decide to rebel? Find yourself the wrong type of man?'

'That's crazy.' She flushed and looked away from those too-penetrating, fabulous bitter-chocolate eyes.

'Is it? Why am I getting a different impression here?'

'I didn't get involved with the wrong type of

guy.' Caroline scoffed nervously. 'I'm not attracted to… This is a silly conversation.'

'Okay, maybe you weren't escaping an ill-
judged, torrid affair with a married man, but what
then? Were the chickens and the sheep and the
village-hall dances every Friday night all a little
too much?'

Caroline looked at him resentfully from under
her lashes and then hurriedly looked away. How
had he managed to turn this conversation on its
head?

'Well?' Giancarlo asked softly, intrigued. 'You
can't make the rules to only suit yourself. Two
can play at this little game of going where you
don't belong…'

'Oh, for goodness' sake! I *may* have become just
a little bored, but so what?' She fidgeted with the
edge of the towel and glared at him, because she
felt like a traitor to her parents with that admission, and it was *his* fault. 'Italy seemed like a brilliant idea,' she admitted, sliding a sideways look
at him, realising that he wasn't smirking as she
might have expected. 'London was just too expensive. You need to have a well-paid job to go there
and actually be able to afford somewhere to rent,

and I didn't want to go to any of the other big cit-
ies. When Dad suggested that he get in touch with
Alberto, that brushing up on my Italian would be
a helpful addition to my CV, I guess I jumped at
the chance. And, once I got here, Alberto and I
just seemed to click.'

'So why the guilty look when I asked?'

'I think Mum and Dad always expected that I'd
stay in the country, live the rural idyll just round
the corner from them, maybe get married to one
of the local lads...'

'They said so?'

'No, but...'

'They would have wanted you to fly the nest.'

'They wouldn't. We're very close.'

'If they wanted to keep you tied to them, they
would never have suggested a move as dramatic
as Italy,' Giancarlo told her drily. 'Trust me, they
aren't fools. This would have been their gentle way of helping you to find your own space.
Shame, though.'

'What do you mean?'

'I was really beginning to warm to the idea of
the unsuitable lover.'

Caroline's breath caught sharply in her throat

because she was registering how close they were to one another, and lying on her side, she felt even more vulnerable to his watchful dark eyes. Conscious of her every movement, she awkwardly sat up and half-wrapped the towel over her legs.

'I… I'm not attracted to unsuitable men,' she croaked, because he appeared to be waiting for a reply to his murmured statement, head slightly inclined.

'Define *unsuitable*…' He lazily reached over to the cooler bag which he had brought with him, and which she had barely noticed in her panic over the dreaded sailing trip, and pulled out two cold drinks, one of which he handed to her.

Held hostage to a conversation that was running wildly out of control, Caroline could only stare at him in dazed confusion. She pressed the cold can to her heated cheeks.

'Well?' Giancarlo tipped his head back to drink and she found that she couldn't tear her eyes away from him, from the motion of his throat as he swallowed and the play of muscles in his raised arm.

'I like kind, thoughtful, sensitive men,' she breathed.

'Sounds boring.'

'It's not boring to like *good guys*, guys who won't let you down.'

'In which case, where are these guys who don't let you down?'

'I'm not in a relationship at the moment, if that's what you're asking,' Caroline told him primly, hoping that he wouldn't detect the flustered catch in her voice.

'No. Good guys can be a crashing disappointment, I should imagine.'

'I'm sure some of your past girlfriends wouldn't agree with that!' Bright patches of colour had appeared on her cheeks, and her eyes were locked to his in a way that was invasive and thrilling at the same time. Had he leant closer to her? Or had she somehow managed to shorten the distance between them?

'I've never had any complaints in that department,' Giancarlo murmured. 'Sure, some of them have mistakenly got it into their heads that they could persuade me to be in it for the long term. Sure, they were disappointed when I had to set them straight on that, but complaints? In the sex department? No. In fact—'

'I'm not interested,' Caroline interrupted shrilly.

Giancarlo dealt her a slashing smile tinged with a healthy dose of disbelief.

'I guess you haven't met a lot of Italian studs out here,' he said, shamelessly fishing and enjoying himself in a way that had become alien to him. His high-pressured, high-octane, high-stressed, driven everyday life had been left behind on the shores of Lake Como. He was playing truant now and loving every second of it. His dark eyes drifted down to her full, heaving breasts. She might have modestly half-covered her bare legs with the towel but she couldn't hide what remained on display, nor could he seem to stop himself from appreciating it.

'I didn't come here to meet anyone! That wasn't the point.'

'No, but it might have been a pleasant bonus—unless, of course, you've left someone behind? Is there a local lad waiting for you in the wings? Someone your parents approve heartily of? Maybe a farmer?'

Caroline wondered why he would have picked a *farmer*, of all people. Was it because he considered her the outdoor kind of girl, robust and healthy with pink cheeks and a hearty appetite? The kind of girl he would never have kissed unless he had been obliged to, as a distraction from the embarrassment of having the girl in question make a fool of herself and of him by having a panic attack at the thought of getting into a boat? She sucked her stomach in, gave up the losing battle to look skinny and stood up to move to the side of the boat, where she held the railings and looked out to the lake.

The shore was a distant strip but she wasn't scared. Just like that, her irrational fear of water seemed to have subsided. There wasn't enough room for that silly phobia when Giancarlo was doing crazy things to her senses. And, much as he got under her skin, his presence was weirdly reassuring. How did *that* work?

She was aware that he had moved to stand behind her and in one swift movement she turned around, her back to the waist-high railing. 'It's so peaceful and beautiful here.' She looked at him steadily and tried hard to focus just on his face rather than on his brown, hard torso and its generous sprinkling of dark hair that seemed horribly, unashamedly masculine. 'Do you miss it? I know Milan is very busy and very commercial, but you grew up here. Don't you sometimes long for the tranquillity of the open spaces?'

'I think you're confusing me with one of those sensitive types you claim to like,' Giancarlo murmured. He clasped the railing on either side of her, bracing himself and locking her into a suffocating, non-physical embrace, his lean body only inches away from her. 'I don't do nostalgia. Not, I might add, that I have much to be nostalgic about.'

The smile he shot her sent a heat wave rushing through her body. She was barefoot and her toes curled against the smooth wooden planks of the sailboat. God, she could scarcely breathe! Their eyes tangled and Caroline felt giddy under the shimmering intensity of his midnight-dark eyes.

She could barely remember what they had been talking about. The quiet sounds of the water had receded and she thought she could hear the whoosh of blood rushing through her veins and the frantic pounding of her heart.

She wasn't aware of her eyes half closing, or of her mouth parting on a question that was never asked.

Giancarlo was more than aware of both those

things. The powerful scent of lust made his nostrils flare. He realised that this was exactly what he wanted. Her lush, sexy body combined with her wide-eyed innocence had set up a chain reaction in him that he hadn't been able to control.

'And as for getting away from it all…' Some of her long hair blew across his face. She smelled of sun and warmth. 'I have a place on the coast.' From nowhere sprang such a strange notion that he barely registered it. He would like to take her there. He had never had any such inclination with any woman in the past. That was purely his domain, his private getaway from the hassle of everyday life, always maintained, waiting and ready for those very rare occasions when he felt the need to make use of it.

'You have the most amazing hair.' He captured some of it, sank his fingers into its untamed length. 'You should never have it cut.'

Caroline knew that he was going to kiss her and she strained up towards him with a sigh of abandon. She never knew that she could want something so much in her life. She lifted her hand and trembled as her fingers raked through his fine, dark, silky hair.

With a stifled groan, Giancarlo angled down and lost himself in a kiss that was hungry and exploring. His questing tongue melded with hers and, as the kiss deepened, he spanned her rib cage with urgent, impatient hands. They were out in the open but visible to no one. Other boats, dotted on the sparkling, still water, were too far away to witness his lack of control.

The push of her breasts as she curved her body up to him was explosive to his libido and he hooked his fingers under the straps of her swim-suit. He couldn't pull them down fast enough, and as her breasts spilled out in their glorious abun-dance he had to control the savage reaction of his throbbing arousal.

'God, you're beautiful,' he growled hoarsely.

'Beautiful' had never been one of those things Caroline had ever considered herself. Friendly, yes. Reasonably attractive, perhaps. But *beautiful*?

Right now, however, as she looked at him with a fevered, slumberous gaze, she believed him and she was infused with a heady, wanton feel-ing of total recklessness. She wanted to bask in his open admiration. It was a huge turn-on. He looked down and her nipples tightened and ached in immediate response. Her ability to think and to reason had been scattered to the four winds and she moaned and arched her back as his big hands covered her breasts, massaging them, pushing them up so that her swollen nipples were offered up to his scorching inspection. The sun on her half-naked body was beautifully warm. She closed her eyes, hands outstretched on the railing on either side of her.

It was a snapshot of an erotic, abundant goddess with her hair streaming back, and Giancarlo lowered his head to close his mouth over the pulsating pink disc of a surrendered nipple.

Reaching down, Caroline curled her fingers into his hair. She felt like a rag doll and had to stop herself from sinking to the floor of the boat as he plundered her breasts, first one then the other, suckling on her nipple, drawing it into his mouth so that he could tease the distended tip with his tongue. She felt powerful and submissive at the same time as he feasted on her, licking, nipping, sucking, driving her crazy with his mouth.

When his hand clasped her thigh, she nearly fainted. The swimsuit was pulled lower and he trailed kisses over each inch of flesh that was gradually exposed. The paleness of her stomach was a sharp contrast to the golden colour she had acquired over the summer months.

Giancarlo found that he liked that. It was a *real* body, the body of a living, breathing, fulsome woman, unlike the statue-perfect, all-over-bronzed bodies of the stick insects he was accustomed to. He rose to his feet and pushed his leg between her thighs, moving it slowly and insistently which made the boat rock ever so slightly. Caroline, with her phobia of water, barely noticed. She was on a different planet and experiencing sensations that were all new and wonderful.

She only surfaced, abruptly and rudely, when the sound of an outboard motor broke through her blurry, cotton-wool haze. She gasped, shocked at her state of undress and mortified at her rebellious body, which had disobeyed every law of self-preservation to flirt perilously with a situation that instinctively screamed danger.

Struggling to free herself, she felt the boat sway and rock under her and she stumbled to rebalance herself.

'What the hell are you doing? You're going to capsize this thing. Stay still!'

He tried to hold her arms as she frantically endeavoured to pull up her swimsuit and hide the shameful spectacle of her nudity.

'How *could* you?' Caroline was shaking like a leaf as she cautiously made her way back to the centre of the boat. Her huge brown eyes were wide with accusation, and Giancarlo, who had never in living memory experienced any form of rejection from a woman, raked his hand impatiently through his hair.

'How could I *what*?'

'You *know* what!'

He took a couple of steps towards her and was outraged when she shrank back. Did she find him *threatening*?

'What I *know*—' his voice was a whiplash, leaving her no leeway to nurse fanciful notions of being seduced against her will '—is that you *wanted* it, and it's no good huddling there like a virtuous maiden whose virginity has been sullied. Snap out of it, Caroline. You practically threw yourself at me.'

'I did no such *thing*,' Caroline whispered, distraught, because she had, she really *had*, and she couldn't for the life of her understand why.

Giancarlo shook his head with such rampant incredulity that she was forced to look away. When she next sneaked a glance at him, it was to see him preparing to sail back to shore. His face was dark with anger.

With agonising honesty, Caroline licked her lips and cleared her throat. It was no good letting this thing fester in simmering silence. She had had a terrible moment of horrifying misjudgement and she would just have to say something.

'I'm sorry,' she said bravely, addressing his profile, which offered nothing by way of encouragement. 'I know I was partly to blame...'

Giancarlo glanced over to her with a brooding scowl. 'How kind of you to rethink your accusation that I was intent on taking advantage of you.'

'I know you weren't! I never meant to imply that. Look...' With urgent consternation, Caroline leaned towards him. 'I don't know what happened. I don't even *like* you! I disapprove of everything about you.'

'*Everything*, Caroline? Let's not labour that statement too much. You might find that you need to retract it.' Not only was Giancarlo furious at her inexplicable withdrawal, when it had been plain to see that she had been as hot and ready for him as he had been for her, but he was more furious with himself for not being able to look at her for fear of his libido going haywire all over again.

'You took me by surprise.'

'Oh, we're back to that old chestnut, are we? I'm the arch-seducer and you're the shrinking violet!'

'It's the heat,' she countered with increasing desperation. 'And the situation. I've never been on the water like this before. Everything must have just been too much.' She continued to look at him earnestly. 'It's *impossible* for me to be attracted to you.' She sought to impose an explanation for her wildly out-of-character behaviour. 'We don't get along at *all* and I disapprove of why you decided to come here to see Alberto. I don't care about money and I've never been impressed by people who think that making money is the most important thing in the world. And, furthermore, I just don't get it with guys who are scared of commitment. I have no respect for them. So…so…'

'So, despite all of that, you still couldn't resist me. What do you think that says?'

'That's what I'm trying to tell you. It doesn't say *anything*!'

Giancarlo detected the horror in her voice and he didn't quite know how to deal with it. He would have made love to her right there, on the boat, and he certainly couldn't think of any other woman who wouldn't have relished the experience. The fact that this woman was intent on treating it as something she had to remove herself from as quickly as possible was frankly an insult of the highest order.

Caroline felt that she was finally in possession of her senses once again. 'I think you'll agree that that unfortunate episode is something we'd best put right behind us. Pretend it never happened.'

'You're attracted to me, Caroline.'

'I'm not. Haven't you listened to a word I've just been saying? I got carried away because I'm here, on a boat, out of my comfort zone. I don't go for men like you. I know you probably find that horribly insulting but it happens to be the truth.'

'You're attracted to me, and the faster you face that the better off you'll be.'

'And how do you figure that out, Giancarlo? How?'

'You've spent your life thinking that the local

lad who enjoys the barn dance on a Saturday and whose greatest ambition is to have three kids and buy a semi-detached house on the street next to where your parents live is your ideal man. Just as you tried to kid yourself that never leaving the countryside was what you wanted out of life. Wrong on both counts. Your head's telling you what you should want, but here I am, a real man, and you just can't help yourself. Don't worry. Amazingly, it's mutual.'

Caroline went white at his brutal summary of everything she didn't want to face. Her behaviour made no sense to her. She didn't approve of him one bit, yet she had succumbed faster than she could ever have dreamt possible.

It was lust, pure and simple, and he wanted to drag that shameful admission out of her because he had an ego the size of a liner and he didn't care for the fact that she had rejected him. Had he thought that he was complimenting her when he told her that, *amazingly*, he found her attractive? Did he seriously think that it felt good to be somebody's novelty for five minutes before he returned to the sort of woman he usually liked?

Warning bells were ringing so loudly in her

head that she would have been a complete idiot not to listen to them. She found that she was gripping the sides of the salty plank of wood sufficiently hard for her knuckles to whiten.

Glancing across at her, Giancarlo could see the slow, painful realisation of the truth sinking in. He had never thought himself the kind of loser who tolerated a woman who blew hot and then blew cold. Women like that were a little too much like hard work. But this woman…

'Okay.' Caroline's words tumbled over one another and she kept her eyes firmly fixed on the fast-approaching shoreline. 'So I find you attractive. You're right. Satisfied? But I'm glad you've dragged that out of me because it's only lust and lust doesn't mean anything. Not to me, anyway. So there. Now it's out in the open and we can both forget about it.'

CHAPTER SIX

IT WAS after five by the time they were finally back at the villa. The outing on the lake had taken much longer than she had thought and then, despite its dramatic conclusion, Giancarlo had insisted on stopping somewhere for them to have a very late lunch.

To add insult to injury, he had proceeded to talk to her as naturally as though nothing had happened between them. He pointed out various interesting landmarks; he gave her an informative lecture on the Vezio Castle, asking her whether she had been there. She hadn't. He seemed to know the history of a lot of the grand mansions, monuments to the rich and famous, and was a fount of information on all the local gossip surrounding the illustrious families.

Caroline just wanted to go home. She was bewildered, confused and in a state of sickening inner turmoil. As he had talked, gesticulating in a way that was peculiarly Italian, she had watched those hands and felt giddy at the thought of where they had been—on her naked body, touching and caressing her in a way that made her breathing quicken and brought a flush of hectic colour to her cheeks. She looked at his sensual mouth as he spoke and remembered in graphic detail the feel of his lips on her breasts, suckling her nipples until she had wanted to scream with pleasure.

How was she supposed to laugh and chat as though none of that had happened?

And yet, wasn't that precisely what she wanted, what she had told him to do—pretend that nothing had happened? Sweep it all under the carpet and forget about it?

She hated the way he could still manage to penetrate her tight-lipped silence to make her smile at something he said. Obviously, *she* was the only one affected by what had happened out there on the lake.

'Thank you for today,' she told him politely as she opened the car door almost before he had had time to kill the engine.

'Which bit of it are you thanking me for?' Giancarlo rested glittering eyes on her and raised his eyebrows in a telling question that made her blush even more ferociously. She was the perfect portrait of a woman who couldn't wait to flee his company. In fact, she had withstood his polite onslaught over an unnecessarily prolonged lunch with the stoicism of someone obliged to endure a cruel and unusual punishment and, perversely, the fiercer her long-suffering expression, the more he had become intent on obliterating it. Now and again he had succeeded, making her laugh even though he could see that she was fighting the impulse.

Giancarlo didn't understand where his reaction to her was coming from.

She had made a great production of telling him just why she couldn't possibly be attracted to a man like him—all lies, of course, as he had proceeded to prove. But she had had a valid point. Where was the common ground between them? She was gauche, unsophisticated and completely lacking in feminine wiles. In short, nothing like the sort of women he went out with. But, hell, she turned him on. She had even managed to turn him on when she had been sitting there, at the little trattoria, paying attention to everyone around them and only reluctantly looking at him when she'd had no choice.

What was that about? Was his ego so inflated that he couldn't abide the thought of wanting a woman and not having instant and willing gratification? It was not in his nature to dwell on anything, to be remotely introspective, so he quickly shelved that thorny slice of self-examination.

Instead, he chose to focus on the reality of the situation. He was here, dragged back to his past by circumstances he could never have foreseen. Although he had a mission to complete, one that had been handed to him on a plate, it was, he would now concede, a mission that would have to be accomplished with a certain amount of subtlety.

In the meantime, reluctant prisoner though he might be, he found himself in the company of a woman who seemed to possess the knack of wreaking havoc with his self-control. What was he to do about it? Like an itch that had to be scratched, Giancarlo found himself in the awkward and novel position of wanting her beyond reason and knowing that he was prepared to go beyond the call of duty to get her. It was frustrating that he knew she wanted him too and was yet reluctant to dip her toes in the water. Heck, they were both adults, weren't they?

Now, faced with a direct question, she stared at him in mute, embarrassed silence.

'I haven't seen as much of the countryside around here as I would have liked,' Caroline returned politely, averting her eyes to stare just behind his shoulder. 'I have a driving licence, and of course Alberto said that I was more than welcome to use the car, but I haven't been brave enough to do much more than potter into the nearest town. Before he fell ill, we did take a couple of drives out for lunch, but there's still so much left to explore.'

Giancarlo smiled back at her through gritted teeth. He wanted to turn her face to him and *make* her look him in the eyes. It got on his nerves the way she hovered, as if waiting for permission to be dismissed.

He also hated the way he could feel himself stirring into unwelcome arousal, getting hard at the sight of her, her soft, ultra-feminine curves and her stubborn, pouting full mouth. He wanted to snatch her to him and kiss her into submission, kiss her until she was begging him to have his way with her. He almost laughed at his sudden caveman-like departure from his normal polished behaviour.

'Any time,' he said shortly and she reluctantly looked at him.

'Oh, thanks very much, but I doubt the occasion will arise again. After all, you're not here for much longer and I'll be returning to my usual routine with Alberto from tomorrow. Do you need a hand taking anything in? It's just that I'm really hot and sticky and dying to have a shower...'

'In that case, off you go. I think I can manage a couple of towels and a cool bag.'

Caroline fled. She intended on ducking into the safety of her room, which would give her time to gather herself. Instead, she opened the front door to be confronted with a freshly laundered Alberto emerging from the kitchens, with Tessa in tow.

He paused in the middle of a testy row, which Tessa was enduring with a broad smile, to look shrewdly at Caroline from under beetling brows.

'Been a long time out there, my girl. What have you been getting up to, eh? You look tousled.'

'Leave the poor woman alone, Alberto. It's none of your business *what* she's been getting up to!'

'I haven't been getting up to *anything*!' Caroline addressed both of them in a high voice. 'I mean, it's been a lovely day out…'

'Sailing? I take it my son managed to cure your fear of water?'

'I…I… Turns out I wasn't as scared of the water as I'd thought. You know how it is…childhood trauma…long story. Anyway, I'm awfully hot and sticky. Are you going to be in the sitting-room, Alberto? Shall I join you there as soon as I've had my shower?'

'Where's Giancarlo?'

'Oh, he's just taking some stuff out of the car.' The devil worked on idle hands, and a day spent lazing around had made Alberto frisky. Caroline could spot that devilish glint in his eyes a mile away and she eyed the staircase behind him with longing.

'So you two got along, then, did you? Wasn't sure if you would, as you seem very different characters, but you know what they say about opposites attracting…' Inquisitive eyes twinkled at her as a tide of colour rose into her face. Next to him, Tessa was rolling her eyes to the ceiling and shooting her a look that said, 'Just ignore him—he's in one of his playful moods.'

'I'm not in the *slightest* attracted to your son!' Caroline felt compelled to set the record straight. 'You're one-hundred percent right. We're completely different, *total* opposites. In fact, I'm *surprised* that I managed to put up with him for such a long time. I suppose I must have been so *engrossed* with the whole sailing business that *I barely noticed* him at all.' By the time she had finished that ringing declaration, her voice was shrill and slightly hoarse. She was unaware of Giancarlo behind her and when he spoke it sent shivers of awareness racing up and down her spine, giving her goose bumps.

'Now, now,' he drawled softly. 'It wasn't as bad as all that, was it, Caroline?'

The way he spoke her name was like a caress. Alberto was looking at them with unconcealed, lively interest. She had to put a stop to this nonsense straight away.

'I never said it was bad. I had a lovely day. Now, if you'll all excuse me…' As an afterthought, she said to Tessa, 'You'll be joining us tonight for dinner, won't you?' But, as luck would have it, Tessa was going to visit her sister and would be back later, in time to make sure that Alberto took his medication—which at least diverted the conversation away from her. She left them to it, with Alberto informing Tessa that he was feeling better and better every day, and he would be in touch with the consultant to see whether he could stop the tablets.

'And then, my dearest harridan, you'll be back to the daily grind at the hospital, tormenting some other poor, innocent soul. You'll miss me, of course, but don't think for a moment that I'll be missing you.' Caroline left him crowing as she hurried towards the staircase.

She took her time having a long, luxurious bath and then carefully choosing what she would wear. Everything, even the most boring and innocuous garments, seemed to be flagrantly revealing. Her tee shirts stretched tautly across her breasts; her jeans clung too tightly to her legs; her blouses were all too low-cut and her skirts made her think how easy it would be for his hand to reach under to the bare skin of her thighs.

In the end she settled for a pair of leggings and a casual black top that screamed 'matronly'.

She found them in the sitting-room where a tense silence greeted her arrival.

Alberto was in his usual position by the window and Giancarlo, on one of the upright chairs, was nursing what looked like a glass of whisky.

Caught off-guard by an atmosphere that was thick and uncomfortable, Caroline hovered by the door until Alberto waved her impatiently in.

'I can't face the dining-room tonight,' he declared, waving at a platter of snacks on the sideboard. 'I got the girl to bring something light for us to nibble on here. For God's sake, woman, stop standing there like a spectre at the feast and help yourself to something to drink. You know where it all is.'

Caroline slid her eyes across to Giancarlo. His long legs were stretched out, lightly crossed at the ankles. For all the world he looked like a man who was completely relaxed, but there was a threatening stillness about him that made her nervous.

She became even more nervous when Alberto said, with a barb to his voice, 'My son and I were just discussing the state of the world. And, more specifically, the state of *my* world, as evidenced in my business interests.'

Giancarlo watched for her reaction with brooding, lazy interest. So the elephant in the room had been brought out into the open. Why not? If the dancing had to begin, why not be the one to start the music instead of waiting? So much easier to be the one in control and, of course, control was a weapon he had always wielded with ruthless efficiency.

'Your colour's up, Alberto,' Caroline said worriedly. She glared at Giancarlo, who returned her stare evenly. 'Perhaps this isn't the right time to...'

'There is no right time or wrong time when it comes to talking about money, my girl. But maybe we should carry on our little *discussion* later, eh, my boy?' He impatiently gestured for Caroline to bring him the tray of snacks but his sharp eyes were on Giancarlo.

So he'd done it, Caroline thought in a daze, he'd *actually* gone and done it. She could feel it in her bones. Giancarlo had tired of dancing around the purpose for his visit to the villa. Maybe her rejection had hastened thoughts of departure and he had decided that this would be as good a time as any to finally achieve what he had intended to achieve from the very start. Perhaps Alberto's declarations of improving health had persuaded Giancarlo that there was no longer any need to beat around the bush. At any rate, Alberto's flushed face and Giancarlo's cool, guarded silence were saying it all.

Caroline felt crushed by the weight of bitter disappointment. She realised that there had been a part of her that had really hoped that Giancarlo would ditch his stupid desire for revenge and move on, underneath the posturing. She had glimpsed the three-dimensional, complex man behind the façade and had dared to expect more. God, she'd been a fool.

She sank into the deepest, most comfortable chair by the sprawling stone fireplace. From there, she was able to witness, in ever-increasing dismay, the awkwardness between father and son. The subject of money was avoided, but it lay unspoken in the air between them, like a Pandora's box waiting for the lid to be opened.

They talked about the sailing trip. Alberto politely asked what it felt like to be back on the water. Giancarlo replied that, of course, it was an unaccustomed pleasure bearing in mind that life in Milan as a boy had not included such luxuries as sailing trips, not when money had been carefully rationed. In a scrupulously polite voice, he asked Alberto about the villa and then gave a little lecture on the necessity for maintenance of an old property because old properties had a nasty habit of falling apart if left unattended for too long. But of course, he added blandly, old places *did* take money… Had he ever thought of leaving or was possession of one of the area's most picturesque properties just too big a feather in his cap?

After an hour and a half, during which time Ella had removed the snacks and replaced them with a pot of steaming coffee, Caroline was no longer able to bear the crushing discomfort of being caught between two people, one of whom had declared war. She stood up, said something polite about Tessa being back soon and yawned; she would be off to bed. With a forced smile, she parroted something to Alberto about making sure he didn't stay up much longer, that he was to call her on her mobile if Tessa was not back within the hour so that she could help him upstairs. She couldn't look at Giancarlo. His brooding silence frightened her.

'You should maybe come up with me.' She gave it her last best shot to avert the inevitable, but Alberto shook his head briskly.

'My son and I have matters to discuss. I can't pretend there aren't one or two things that need sorting out, and might as well sort them out now. I've never been one to run from the truth!' He was addressing Caroline but staring at Giancarlo. 'It's much better to get the truth out than let things fester.'

Caroline imagined the showdown—well, in Giancarlo's eyes, it was a showdown that had been brewing for the best part of his life and he had come prepared to win it at all costs. She was being dismissed but still she hesitated, searching valiantly for some miracle she could produce from nowhere, like a magician pulling a rabbit from a hat. But there was no miracle and she retreated upstairs. The villa was so extensive that there was no way she could possibly pick up the sound of raised voices, nor could she even hear whether Tessa had returned or not to rescue Alberto from his own son.

She fell into a fitful sleep and awoke with a start to the moon slanting silver light through the window. She had been reading and her book had dropped to the side of the bed. It took a few seconds for her eyes to adjust to the darkness and a few more seconds for her to remember what had been worrying her before she had nodded off: Alberto and Giancarlo. The unbearable tension, like a storm brewing in the distance, waiting to erupt with devastating consequences.

Groaning, she heaved herself out of the four-poster bed, slipped on her dressing gown and headed downstairs, although she wasn't quite sure what she expected to find.

Alberto's suite of rooms lay at the far end of the long corridor, beyond the staircase. Hesitating at the top of the winding staircase, Caroline was tempted to check on him, but first she would go downstairs, make sure that the two of them weren't still locked in a battle to the bitter end. Truth, as Alberto had declared, was something that could take hours to hammer out—and in this case the outcome would be certain defeat for Alberto. He would finally have to bow to Giancarlo and put his destiny in his hands. With financial collapse at his door, what other alternative would there be?

She arrived at the sitting-room to see a slither of light under the shut door. Although she couldn't hear any voices, what else could that light mean except that they were both still in the room? She pushed open the door before she could do what she really wanted to do, which was to run away.

The light came from one of the tall standard lamps that dotted the large room. Sprawled on the chair with his head flung back, eyes closed and a drink cradled loosely in one hand, Giancarlo looked heart-stoppingly handsome and, for once, did not appear to be a man at the top of his game. His hair was tousled, as though he had raked his fingers through it too many times, and he looked ashen and exhausted.

She barely made a sound, but he opened his eyes immediately, although it seemed to take him a few seconds before he could focus on her, and when he did he remained where he was, slumped in the chair.

'Where is Alberto?'

Giancarlo swirled the liquid in his glass without answering and then swallowed back the lot without taking his eyes from her face.

'How much have you *drunk*, Giancarlo?' Galvanised into sudden action, Caroline walked briskly towards him. 'You look terrible.'

'I love a woman who tells it like it is.'

'And you haven't told me where Alberto is.'

'I assure you, he isn't hiding anywhere in this room. You have just me for the pleasure of your company.'

Caroline managed to extract the glass from him. 'You need sobering up.'

'Why? Is there some kind of archaic house rule that prohibits the consumption of alcohol after a certain time?'

'Wait right here. I'm going to go and make a pot of coffee.'

'You have my word. I have no intention of going anywhere, any time soon.'

For once, Caroline failed to be awed by the size and grandeur of the villa. For once, she wished that the kitchens didn't involve a five-minute hike through winding corridors and stately reception rooms. She could barely contain her nerves as she anxiously waited for the kettle to boil, and by the time she made it back to the sitting-room, burdened with a tray on which was piled a mound of buttered toast and a very large pot of black, strong coffee, she half-expected to find that Giancarlo had disappeared.

He hadn't. He had managed to refill his glass and she gently but firmly removed it from him, brought the tray over to place it on the oval table by his chair and then pulled one of the upright, velvet-covered stools towards him.

'What are you doing here, anyway? Did you come down to make sure that the duel at dawn hadn't begun?'

'You should eat something, Giancarlo.' She urged a slice of toast on him and he twirled it thoughtfully between his fingers, examining it as though he had never seen anything like it before.

'You are a very caring person, Caroline Rossi, but I expect you've been told that before. I can't imagine too many women preparing me toast and coffee because they were worried that I'd drunk too much. Although...' He half-leaned towards her, steadying himself on the arm of his chair. 'I've never drunk too much—least of all when in the company of a woman.' He bit into the toast with apparent relish and settled his lustrous dark eyes on her.

'So, what happened? I don't mean to pry…'

'Of course you mean to pry.' He half-closed his eyes, shifted a little in the chair, indicated that he wanted more toast and drank some of the very strong coffee. 'You have my father's welfare at heart.'

'We can talk in the morning, when you're feeling a little less, um, worse for wear.'

'It would take more than half a bottle of whisky to make me feel worse for wear. I've the constitution of an ox. I made a mistake.'

'I know. Well. That's what people always say after they've drunk too much. They also say that they'll never do it again.'

'You're not following me. I made a *mistake*. I screwed up.'

'Giancarlo, I don't know what you're talking about.'

'Of course you don't. Why should you? To summarise—you were right and I was wrong.' He rubbed his eyes, sighed heavily, thought about standing up and discovered that he couldn't be bothered. 'I came here hell-bent on setting the record straight. There were debts to be settled. I was going to be the debt collector. Well, here's one for the book—the invincible Giancarlo didn't get his facts straight.'

'What do you mean?'

'I was always led to believe that Alberto was a bitter ex-husband who had ensured that my mother got as little as possible in her divorce settlement. I was led to believe that he was a monster who had walked away from a difficult situation, having made sure that my mother suffered for the temerity of having a mind of her own. I was drip-fed a series of half-truths! I think another glass of whisky might help the situation.'

'It won't.'

'You told me that there might be another side to the story.'

'There always is.' Her heart constricted in sympathy. Unused to dealing with any kind of emotional doubt, Giancarlo had steadily tried to drink his way out of it. More than anything in the world, Caroline wanted to reach out and smooth away the lines of bitter self-recrimination from his beautiful face.

'My mother had been having affairs. By the

time the marriage dissolved, she was involved with a man who turned out to be a con artist. There was a massive settlement. My mother failed to do anything with it. Instead, she handed it over to a certain Bertoldo Monti who persuaded her that he could treble what she'd had. He took the lot and disappeared. Alberto showed me all the documents, the letters my mother wrote begging for more money. Well, he carried on supporting her, and in return she refused to let him see me. She informed him that I was settled, that I didn't want contact. Letters he sent me were returned unopened. He kept them all.'

Giancarlo's voice was raw with emotion. Caroline could feel tears begin to gather at the back of her eyes and she blinked them away, for the last thing a man as proud as Giancarlo would want would be any show of sympathy. Not now, not when his eyes had been ripped open to truths he had never expected.

'I expect that the only reason I received the top education that I did was because the money was paid directly to the school. It was one of those *basics* that Alberto made sure were covered be-cause, certainly, there seems little question that my mother would have spent it or given it away to one of her many lovers, had she had it in her possession.'

'I'm sure, in her own way, she never thought that what she was doing was bad.'

'Ever the cheerful optimist, aren't you?' He laughed harshly, but when he looked at her, his eyes were wearily amused. 'So, it would seem, is my father. Do you know, I used to wonder what you had in common with Alberto. He was a bitter and twisted old man with no time for anyone but himself. You were young and innocent. Seems you two have more in common than I ever imagined. He, too, told me the same thing—my mother was unhappy. He worked too hard. She was bored. He blamed himself for not being around sufficiently to build up a relationship with me and she took advantage of that. She took advantage of his pride, threatened to air all their dirty linen in public if he tried to pursue custody, convinced him that he had failed as a father and that visits would be pointless and disruptive. I was her trump card and she used me to get back at him.

'God, do you know that when she died, Alberto requested to see me via a lawyer and I knocked him back? She behaved badly, she warped my attitudes, but the truth is she was a simple waitress who was plucked from obscurity and deposited into a lifestyle with which she was unfamiliar and ill at ease. The whole thing was a mess. *Is* still a mess. Alberto didn't know the extent of his financial losses. He's relied on his trusted accountant for the past ten years and he's been kept pretty much in the dark about the true nature of the company accounts. Of course, like a bull in a china shop, that was one of my choice opening observations.'

'Stop blaming yourself, Giancarlo. You were a child when you left here. You weren't to know that things weren't as they seemed. Was…was Alberto okay when he heard? I guess in a way it's quite a good thing that you came along to tell him, because if you hadn't none of these secrets would have ever emerged. He's old. How good is it for the two of you that all these truths have come out? How much better for you both to have reached a place where new beginnings can start, even though the price you've both paid has been so high?'

This time Giancarlo offered her a crooked smile. 'I suppose that's one upbeat way of looking at it.'

'And I know the situation between you hasn't been *ideal*, but when it comes to Alberto and the money, how much worse for him to have been called into an impersonal office somewhere, told that everything he'd spent your life working for had been washed down the tubes?'

'As things turn out.' He closed his eyes briefly, giving her some stolen moments to savour the harsh, stunning contours of his face. Seeing him like this, vulnerable and flawed but brutally, fiercely honest with himself, did something strange inside her. A part of her seemed to connect with him in a way that was scary and thrilling.

'As things turn out?' she prompted, while her mind drifted to things going on in her head that made her heart beat faster and her pulses race. Could she be *falling* for the guy? Surely not? She would be crazy to do something like that, and she wasn't crazy. But he made her feel *alive*, took her to a different level where all her emotions and senses were amplified in a way that was new and dangerous but also wonderful.

'As things turn out, reparation is long overdue. I don't blame my mother for the things she did. She was who she was, and I have to accept my own portion of responsibility for failing to question when I was old enough to do so.' He held his hand up as though to forestall an argument, although the last thing Caroline was about to do was argue with him. First and foremost, she wanted to get her thoughts in order. She looked at him with a slightly glazed expression.

'Right,' she said slowly, blinking and nodding her head thoughtfully. She noticed that, even having been at the bottle, he was still in control of all his faculties, still able to rationalise his thoughts in a way that many sober people couldn't. He might be ruthless with others who didn't meet his high standards, but he was also ruthless with himself, and that was an indication of his tremendous honesty and fairness. Throw killer looks into the mix, and was it any wonder that her silly, inexperienced head had been well and truly turned? Surely that natural reaction could not be confused with love.

'The least I can do—' he murmured in such a low voice that she had to strain to hear him '—and I have told Alberto this—is to get people in to sort out the company. Old friends and stalwarts are all well and good, but it appears that they have allowed time to do its worst. Whatever it takes, it will be restored to its former glory and an injection of new blood will ensure that it remains there. And there will be no transfer of title. My father will continue to own his company, along with his villa, which I intend to similarly restore.'

Caroline smiled without reservation. 'I'm so glad to hear that, Giancarlo.'

'You mean, you aren't going say "I told you so", even though you did?'

'I would never say anything like that.'

'Do you know, I'm inclined to believe you.'

'I'm really glad I came downstairs,' she confessed honestly. 'It took me ages to fall asleep and then I woke up and wanted to know that everything was all right, but I wasn't sure what to do.'

'Would you believe me if I told you that I'm glad you came downstairs too?'

Caroline found that she was holding her breath. He was staring at her with brooding intensity and she couldn't drag her fascinated eyes away from his face. Without realising it, she was leaning forwards, every nerve in her body straining towards him, like a flower reaching towards a source of heat and light.

'Really?'

'Really,' Giancarlo said wryly. 'I'm not the sort of man who thinks there's anything to be gained by soul searching but you appear to have a talent for listening.'

'And, also, drink lowers inhibitions,' Caroline felt compelled to add, although she was flushed with pleasure.

'This is true.'

'So what happens next?' Caroline asked breathlessly. She envisaged him heading off to sort out companies and a bottomless void seemed to open up at her feet. 'I mean, are you going to be leaving soon?' she heard herself ask.

'For once, work is going to be put on hold.' Giancarlo looked at her lazily. 'I have a house on the coast.'

'So you said.'

'A change of scenery might well work wonders with Alberto and it would give us time to truly put an uncomfortable past behind us.'

'And would I stay here to look after the villa?'

'Would that be what you wanted?'

'No! I…I need to be with Alberto. It's part of my job, you know, to make sure that he's okay.' Silence descended. Into it, memories of that passing passion on the boat dropped until her head was filled with images of them together. Her pupils dilated and she couldn't say a word. She was dimly aware that she was shamelessly staring at him, way beyond the point of politeness.

She was having an out-of-body experience. At least, that was what it seemed like and so it felt perfectly natural to reach out, just extend her hand a little and trace the outline of his face.

'Don't touch, Caroline.' He continued to look at her with driving intensity. 'Unless you're prepared for the consequences. Are you?'

CHAPTER SEVEN

CAROLINE propped herself up on one elbow and stared at Giancarlo. He was dozing. Due to the throes of love-making, the sheets had become a wildly crumpled silken mass that was draped half-on, half-off the bed, and in the silvery moonlight, his long, muscular limbs in repose were like the silhouettes of a perfectly carved fallen statue. She itched to touch them. Indeed, she could feel the tell-tale throb between her legs and the steady build-up of dampness that longed for the touch of his mouth, his hands, his exploring fingers.

He had asked her, nearly a fortnight ago, whether she was prepared for the consequences. Yes! Caroline hadn't thought twice. Of course, that first time—and, heck, it seemed like a million years ago—they hadn't made love. Not properly. He was scrupulous when it came to contraception. No, they had touched each other and she had never known that touching could be so mind-blowing.

He had licked every inch of her body, had teased her with his tongue, invaded every private inch of her until she had wanted to pass out.

For Caroline, there had been no turning back.

The few days originally planned by Giancarlo for his visit had extended into two weeks and counting, for he had taken it upon himself to personally oversee the ground changes that needed to be made to Alberto's company. With the authority of command, he had snapped his fingers and in had marched an army of his loyal workforce, who had been released into the company like ants, to work their magic. They stayed at one of the top hotels in the nearby town while Giancarlo remained at the villa, taking his time to try and rebuild a relationship that had been obliterated over time. He would vanish for much of the day, returning early evening, where a routine of sorts had settled into place.

Alberto would always be found in his usual favourite chair in the sitting-room, where Giancarlo would join him for a drink, while upstairs Caroline would ready herself with pounding heart for that first glimpse of Giancarlo of the day.

Alberto didn't suspect a thing. It was in Caroline's

nature to be open and honest, and she was guiltily aware that what she was enjoying was anything but a straightforward relationship. The fact that she and Giancarlo had met under very strange circumstances and that, were it not for those strange circumstances, their paths would never have been destined to cross, was an uneasy truth always playing at the back of her mind. She preferred not to dwell on that, however. What was the point? From that very moment when she had closed her eyes and offered her lips to him, there had been no going back.

So late at night, with Alberto safely asleep, she would creep into Giancarlo's bedroom, or he would come to her, and they would talk softly, make love and then make love all over again like randy teenagers who couldn't get enough of one another.

'You're staring at me.' Giancarlo had always found it irritating when women stared at him, as though he was some kind of poster-boy pin-up, the equivalent of the brainless blonde bimbo. He had found, though, that he could quite happily bask in Caroline's openly appreciative gaze. When they were with Alberto and he felt her eyes slide surreptitiously over him, it was a positive turn-on. On more than one occasion he had had to fight the desire to drag her from the room and make love to her wherever happened to be convenient, even if it was a broom cupboard under the stairs. Not that such a place existed in the villa.

'Was I?'

'I like it. Shall I give you a bit more to stare at?' Lazily, he shrugged off the sheet so that his nakedness was fully exposed and Caroline sighed softly and shuddered.

With a groan of rampant appreciation, Giancarlo reached out for her and felt her willingly fall into his arms. He opened his eyes, pulled her on top of him and ground her against him so that she could feel the rock-hard urgency of his erection. As she propped herself up on his chest, her long hair tumbled in a curtain around her heart-shaped face. Roving eyes took in the full pout of her mouth, the sultry passion in her eyes, the soft swing of her generous breasts hanging down, big nipples almost touching his chest.

What was it about this woman's body that drove him to distraction?

They had made love only an hour before and he

was ready to go again; incredible. He pulled her down to him so that he could kiss her, and now she no longer needed any prompting to move her body in just the right way so that he felt himself holding on by a slither.

'You're a witch,' he growled, tumbling her under him in one easy move, and Caroline smiled with satisfaction, like the cat that not only had got the cream but had managed to work out where there was an unlimited supply.

He pushed her hair back so that he could sweep kisses along her neck while she squirmed under him.

The thrill of anticipation was running through her like a shot of adrenaline. She couldn't seem to get enough of his mouth on her, and as he closed his lips around one nipple she moaned softly and fell back, arms outstretched, to receive the ministrations of his tongue playing against the erect bud of her nipple. She arched back and curled her fingers in his hair as he sucked and suckled, teasing and nipping until the dampness between her legs became pleasurably painful.

She wrapped her legs around him and as he

began moving against her she gave a little cry of satisfaction.

They had arrived at his house on the coast only two days previously, and although it wasn't nearly as big as the villa it was still big enough to ensure perfect privacy when it came to being noisy. Alberto and Tessa were in one wing of the house, she and Giancarlo in the other. It was an arrangement that Caroline had been quick to explain, pointing out in too much detail that it was far more convenient for Tessa to be readily at hand, and the layout of the villa predicated those sleeping arrangements. She had been surprised when Alberto had failed to put up the expected argument, simply shrugging his shoulders and waving her lengthy explanation away.

'Not so fast, my sexy little witch.' Giancarlo paused in his ministrations to stare down at her bare breasts, which never failed to rouse a level of pure primal lust he had hitherto not experienced with any other woman. The circular discs of her nipples were large and dark and he could see the paleness of her skin where the sun hadn't reached. It was incredibly sexy. He leant down and licked the underside of her breasts, enjoying the feel of their weight against his face, then he traced a path down her flat stomach to circle her belly button with his tongue. She was salty with perspiration, as he was, even though it was a cool night and the background whirr of the fan was efficiently circulating the air.

Caroline breathed in sharply, anticipating and thrilling to what was to come, then releasing her breath in one long moan as his tongue flicked along the pulsating sensitised tip of her clitoris, endlessly repeating the motion until she wanted to scream.

In a mindless daze, she looked down at the dark head buried between her thighs and the eroticism of the image was so powerful that she shuddered.

She could barely endure the agony of waiting as, finally, he slipped on protection and entered her in a forceful thrust that sent waves of blissful sensation crashing through her. His hands were under her buttocks as he continued to drive into her, his motions deep and rhythmic. The wave of sensation peaked, and she stiffened and whimpered, her eyes fluttering shut as she was carried away to eventually sag, pleasurably sated, on the bed next to him.

Similarly spent, Giancarlo rolled off her and lay flat, one arm splayed wide, the other clasped around her.

Not for the first time, Caroline was tempted to ask him where they were going, what lay around the corner for the two of them. Surely something that was as good as this wasn't destined to end?

And just as quickly she bit back the temptation. She had long given up on the convenient delusion that what she felt for Giancarlo was nothing more than a spot of healthy lust. Yes, it was lust, but it was lust that was wrapped up in love—and instinctively she knew that love, insofar as it applied to Giancarlo, was a dangerous emotion, best not mentioned.

All she could do was hope that day by day she was becoming an indispensable part of his life.

Certainly, they enjoyed each other's company. He made her laugh and he had told her countless times that she was unique. Unique and beautiful. Surely that meant something?

She steered clear of perilous thoughts to say drowsily, 'I've got to get back to my room. It's late and I'm really, really tired…'

'Too tired for a bath?'

Caroline giggled and shifted in little movements so that she was curled against him. 'Your baths are not good for a girl who needs to get to sleep.'

'Now, what would make you say that?' But he grinned at her as she delicately hid a yawn.

'Not many women fall asleep on me,' he said sternly and she smiled up at him.

'Is that because you tell them that they're not allowed to?'

'It's because they never get the chance. I've never been a great fan of post-coital situations.'

'Why is that?' Thin ice stretched out in front of her because she knew that she could easily edge towards a conversation that might be off-limits with him. 'Is that because too much conversation equals too much involvement?'

'What's brought this on?'

Caroline shrugged and flopped back against the pillows. 'I just want to know if I'm another in a long line of women you sleep with but aren't really involved with.'

'I'm not about to get embroiled in a debate on this. Naturally, I've conversed with the women I've dated. Over dinner. After dinner. On social occasions. But my time after we've made love has been for me. I've never encouraged lazing around between the sheets chatting about nothing in particular.'

'Why not? And don't tell me that I ask too many questions. I'm just curious, that's all.'

'Remember what they say about curiosity and cats…'

'Oh, forget it!' Caroline suddenly exploded. 'It was just a simple question. You get so defensive if someone asks you something you don't want to hear.'

Giancarlo discovered that his gut instinct wasn't to ditch the conversation, even though he didn't like where it was going. What did she expect him to say?

'Maybe I've never found the woman I wanted to have chats with in bed…' he murmured softly, drawing her back to him and feeling her relent in his arms. 'Let's not argue,' he said persuasively. 'This riviera is waiting to be explored.'

'Are you sure you can take all that time off work?'

'Surprisingly, I'm beginning to realise the considerable benefits of the World Wide Web. My father may be a dinosaur when it comes to anything technological, but it's working wonders for me. Almost as good as being at an office but with the added advantage of having a sexy woman I can turn to whenever I want.' He smoothed his big hands along her waist then up to gently caress the softness of one of her breasts.

'*And* you're teaching him.' Caroline was glad to put that moment of discomfort behind them. Questions might be jostling for room in her head but she didn't want to argue. She didn't want to explore the outcome of any arguments. 'He's really enjoying those lessons,' she confided, running her hand along his shoulder and liking the hard feel of muscle and sinew. 'I think he finds the whole experience of having a son rather wonderful. In fact, I know *you* feel maybe a bit guilty that you lived with a past that wasn't quite what you thought it was, but he feels guilty too.'

'He's told you that?'

'He called himself a proud old fool the other day when we were out in the garden, which is his way of regretting that he never got in touch with you over the years.' She glanced behind Giancarlo to where the clock on the ornate bedside table was informing her that it was nearly two in the morning. Her eyelids felt heavy. Should she just grab fifteen minutes of sleep before she trudged back to her bedroom? The warmth of Giancarlo's body next to her dulled her senses but she began edging her way out of the bed.

'Stay,' he urged, pulling her back to him.

'Don't be silly.' Caroline yawned.

'Alberto doesn't get up until at least eight in the morning and by the time he gets his act together it's more like nine-thirty before he makes an appearance in the breakfast room. You can be up at seven and back in your room by five past.' He grinned wolfishly at her. 'And isn't the thought of early-morning sex tempting…?' The suggestion had come from nowhere. If he didn't encourage after-sex chat, he'd never encouraged any woman to stay the night. In fact, no one ever had.

He was playing truant from his real life. At least, that was what it felt like, and why shouldn't he enjoy the time out, at least for a little while? Having been driven all his adult life, having poured all his energies into the business of making money, which had been an ambition silently foisted onto him by his mother, why the hell shouldn't he now take time out under these extraordinary circumstances?

Neither he nor his father had been inclined to indulge in lengthy, analytical conversations about the past. In time and at leisure, they could begin to fill in the gaps, and Giancarlo was looking forward to that. For the moment, Alberto had explained what needed to be explained, and his scattered reminiscences had built a picture of sorts for Giancarlo, a more balanced picture than the one he had been given as a child growing up, but the blame game hadn't been played. After an initial surge of anger at his mother and at himself, Giancarlo was now more accepting of the truth that the past couldn't be changed and so why beat himself up over the unchangeable?

However, he could afford to withdraw from the race for a few weeks, and he wanted to. If Alberto had lost his only child for all those years, then Giancarlo had likewise been deprived of his father and it was a space he was keen to fill. Slowly, gradually, with them both treading the same path of discovery and heading in the same direction.

His thoughts turned to Caroline, so much a part of the complex tableau…

Acting out of character by asking her to spend the night with him was just part and parcel of his time out.

He could feel her sleepily deliberating his proposal. To help her along with her decision, he curved one big hand over her breast and softly massaged the generous swell. Tired she might very well be, and spent after their urgent, hungry love-making, but still her nipple began to swell and pulse as he gently rolled his thumb over the tip.

'Not fair,' Caroline murmured.

'Since when would you expect me to play fair?'

'You can't always get what you want.'

'Why not? Don't you want to wake up in the morning with me touching you like this? Or like this?' He slid his hand down to the damp patch between her legs and slowly stroked her, on and on until she felt her breathing begin to quicken.

Giancarlo watched her face as he continued to pleasure her, enjoyed her heightened colour and then, a whole lot more, enjoyed her as she moved against his fingers, her body gently grinding until she came with a soft, startled gasp.

There seemed to be no end to his enjoyment

of her body and he had ceased to question the strange pull she had over him. He just knew that he wanted her here with him in his bed because he wanted to wake up next to her.

'Okay. You win and I lose.' Caroline sighed. She shouldn't. She knew that. She was just adding to the house of cards she had fabricated around herself. She loved him and it was just so easy to overlook the fact that the word *love* had never crossed his lips. It shamed her to think how glad she was to have him, whatever the price she would have to pay later.

He kissed her eyelids shut; she was *so* tired…

The next time Caroline opened her eyes, it was to sunshine pouring through the open slats of the wooden shutters. She swam up to full consciousness and to the weight of Giancarlo's arm sprawled possessively over her breasts. Their tangled nakedness galvanised her into immediate action and she leapt out of the bed as he groggily came to and tried to tug her back down to him.

'Giancarlo!' she said with dismay. 'It's after seven! I have to go!'

Fully awake, Giancarlo slung his long legs over the side of the bed and killed the instinct to drag her back to him, to hell with the consequences. She was anxiously scouring the ground for her clothes and he sat for a while on the side of the bed to watch her.

'Are you looking for these, by any chance?' He held up her bra, a very unsexy cotton contraption which led him to think that he would quite like to buy her an entirely new set of lingerie, stuff that he would personally choose, sexy, lacy stuff that would look great on her fabulously lush body.

Caroline tried to swipe them and missed as he whipped them just out of reach.

'You'll have to pay a small penalty charge if you want your bra,' he chided. Sitting on the edge of the bed with her standing in front of him put her at just the perfect height for him to nuzzle her breast.

'We haven't got time!' She tried to slap him away and grab her bra, but put up next to no struggle when he yanked her on top of him and rolled her back on the bed.

'I'll shock you at how fast I can be.'

Fast and just as blissfully, sinfully satisfying. It was past seven-thirty as Caroline quietly opened the bedroom door.

She knew that she was unnecessarily cautious

because Giancarlo was right when he had pointed out that his father was a late riser. Very early on in her stay, Alberto had told her that he saw no point in rushing in the morning.

'Lying in bed for as long as you want in the morning,' he had chuckled, 'is the happy prerogative of the teenager and the old man like myself. It's just about the only time I feel like a boy again!'

So the very last thing she expected as she opened the door and let herself very quietly out of Giancarlo's bedroom was to hear Alberto say from behind her, 'And what do we have *here*, my dear?'

Caroline froze and then turned around. She could feel the hot sting of guilt redden her cheeks. Alberto, walking stick in hand, was looking at her with intense curiosity.

'Correct me if I'm wrong, but isn't that my *son's* bedroom?'

He invested the word *bedroom* with such heavy significance that Caroline was lost for words.

'I thought you would still be asleep,' was all she could manage to dredge from her befuddled mind. He raised his bushy eyebrows inquisitively.

'Do you mean that you *hoped* I would still be asleep?'

'Alberto, I can explain…'

As she racked her brains to try and come up with an explanation, she was not aware of Giancarlo quietly opening the bedroom door she had previously shut behind her.

'No point. My father wasn't born yesterday. I'm sure he can jump to all the right conclusions.'

As if to underline his words, Caroline spun round to find that Giancarlo hadn't even bothered to get dressed. He had stuck on his dressing gown, a black silk affair which was only loosely belted at the waist. Was he wearing anything *at all* underneath? she wondered, subduing a frantic temptation to laugh like a maniac. Or would some slight shift expose him in all his wonderful naked glory? Surely not.

The temptation to laugh gave way to the temptation to groan out loud and bash her head against the wall.

Alberto was looking between them. 'I'm not sure how to deal with this shock,' he said weakly, glancing around him for support and finally settling on the dado rail. 'This is not what I expected from either of you!'

'I'm so sorry.' Caroline's voice was thin and pleading. She was suddenly very ashamed of herself. She was in her twenties and yet she felt like a teenager being reprimanded.

'Son, I'll be honest with you—I'm very disappointed.' He shook his head sadly on a heavy sigh and Giancarlo and Caroline remained where they were, stunned. Giancarlo, however, was the first to snap out of it. He took two long strides down the corridor, where a balmy early-morning breeze rustled against the louvres and made the pale voile covering them billow provocatively.

'Papa…'

Alberto, who had turned away, stopped in his unsteady progress back to his wing of the house and tilted his head to one side.

Giancarlo too temporarily paused. It was the first time he had used that word, the first time he had called him 'Papa' as opposed to Alberto.

'Look, I know what you're probably thinking.' Giancarlo raked his fingers through his bed-tousled hair and shook his head in frustration.

'I very much doubt you do, son,' Alberto said

mournfully. 'I know I'm a little old-fashioned when it comes to these things, and I do realise that this is your house and you are a grown man fully capable of making his own rules under his own roof, but just tell me this—how long? How long has this been going on? Were you two misbehaving while you were in the villa?'

'*Misbehaving* is not exactly what I would term it,' Giancarlo said roughly, his face darkly flushed, but Alberto was looking past him to where Caroline was dithering on legs that felt like jelly by the louvred window.

'When your parents sent you over to Italy, I very much think that this is not the sort of thing they would have expected,' he told her heavily, which brought on another tidal wave of excruciating guilt in her. 'They entrusted your well-being to me, and by that I'm sure they were not simply referring to your nutritional well-being.'

'Papa, enough.' Giancarlo plunged his hands into the deep pockets of his dressing gown. 'Caroline's well-being is perfectly safe with me. We are both consenting adults and...'

'Pah!' Alberto waved his hand impatiently.

'We're not idiots who haven't stopped to consider the consequences.' Giancarlo's voice was firm and steady and Alberto narrowed his eyes on his son.

'Carry on.'

Caroline was mesmerised. She had inched her way forwards, although Giancarlo's back was still to her, a barrier against the full force of Alberto's disappointment.

'I may have been guilty in the past of fairly random relationships…' Just one confidence shared with his father after several drinks. 'But Caroline and I…er…have something different.' He glanced over his shoulder towards her. 'Don't we?'

'Um?'

'In fact, only yesterday we were discussing where we were going with what we have here…'

'Ah. You mean that you're serious? Well, that's a completely different thing. Caroline, I feel I know you well enough to suspect that you're the marrying kind of girl. I'm taking it that marriage no less is what we're talking about here?' He beamed at them, while a few feet away Caroline's jaw dropped open and she literally goggled like a goldfish.

'Marriage changes everything. I might be old

but I'm not unaware of the fact that young people are, shall we say, a little more experimental before marriage than they were in my day. I can't believe you two never breathed a word of this to me.'

He chose to give them no scope for interruption. 'But I have eyes in my head, my boy! Could tell from the way you're relaxed here, a changed man, not to put too fine a point on it. And, as for Caroline, well, she's so skittish when she's around you. All the signs were there. I can't tell you what this means to me, after my brush with the grim reaper!'

'Er, Alberto…'

'You get to my age and you need to have something to hold on to, especially after my heart attack. In fact, I think I might need to rest just now after all this excitement. I wish you'd told me instead of letting me find out for myself, not that the end result isn't the same!'

'We didn't say anything because we didn't want to unduly excite you.' Giancarlo strolled back to her and proceeded to sling his arm over her shoulder, dislodging the robe under which he was thankfully decently clad in some silk boxers. 'It's

been a peculiar time, why muddy the waters unnecessarily?'

'Yes, I see that!' Alberto proclaimed with an air
of satisfaction. 'I'm thrilled. You must know by
now, Giancarlo, that I think the world of your fiancée. Can I call you that now, my dear?'

Fiancée? Engaged? Getting married? Had she
been transported into some kind of freaky paral-
lel universe?

'We were going to break it to you over dinner
tonight,' Giancarlo announced with such confidence that Caroline could only marvel at his capacity for acting. How much deeper was he going
to dig this hole? she wondered.

'Of course, you two will want to have some
time off to do the traditional thing—buy a ring.
I could come with you,' Alberto tacked on hopefully. 'I know it's a private and personal thing,
but I can't think of a single thing that would fill
me with more of a sense of hope and optimism,
a reason for *going on*.'

'A reason for going on where?' Tessa demanded,
striding up towards them. 'You're worse than a
puppy off a leash, Alberto! I told you to wait for

me and I would help you down to the breakfast room.'

'Do I look as though I need help, woman?' He waggled his cane at her. 'Another week and I won't even need this damnable piece of tomfoolery to get around! And, not that it's part of your job description to be nosing around, but these two love birds are going to be married!'

'When?' Tessa asked excitedly, while she did something with Alberto's shirt, tried to rearrange the collar; predictably he attempted to shoo her away.

'Good question, my shrewish nurse. Have you two set a date yet?'

Finally, Caroline's tongue unglued itself from the roof of her mouth. She stepped out of Giancarlo's embrace and folded her arms. 'No, we certainly haven't, Alberto. And I think we should stop talking about this. It's…um…still in the planning stage.'

'You're right. We'll talk later, perhaps over a dinner, something special.' Alberto glowered at Tessa, who smiled serenely back at him. 'Get in a couple of bottles of the finest champagne, woman, and don't even think of giving me your "demon drink" lecture. Tonight we celebrate and I fully intend to have a glass with something drinkable in it when we make a toast!'

'Okay,' Giancarlo said, once his father and Tessa had safely disappeared down the stairs and out towards the stunning patio that overlooked the crystal-clear blue of the sea from its advantageous perch on the side of the hill. 'So what else was I supposed to do? I feel like I'm meeting my father for the first time. How could I jeopardise his health, ruin his excitement? You heard him, this gives him something to cling to.'

Caroline felt as though she had done several stomach-churning loops on a roller-coaster which had slackened speed, but only temporarily, with the threat of more to come over the horizon.

'What else were you *supposed to do*?' she parroted incredulously. Engagement? Marriage? All the stuff that was so important to her, stuff that she took really seriously, was for Giancarlo no more than a handy way of getting himself out of an awkward situation.

'My mother slept around,' Giancarlo told her abruptly, flushing darkly. 'I knew she wasn't the most virtuous person on the face of the earth. She was never afraid of introducing her lovers to me but she was single, destroyed after a bad marriage, desperate for love and affection. Little did I know at the time that her capacity for sleeping around had started long before her divorce. She was very beautiful and very flighty. My father refrained from using the word *amoral*, but I'm guessing that that's what he thought.

'Here I am now. The estranged son back on the scene. I'm trying to build something out of nothing because I want a relationship with my father. Finding out that we're sleeping together, him thinking that it's nothing but a fly-by-night romance, well, how high do you think his opinion is going to be of me? How soon before he begins drawing parallels between me and my mother?'

'That's silly,' Caroline said gently. 'Alberto's not like that.' But how far had Giancarlo come? It wasn't that long ago that he had agreed to see Alberto purely for the purpose of revenge. He felt himself on fragile ground now. His plans had unravelled on all sides, truths had been exposed and a past rewritten. She could begin to see why he would do anything within his power not to jeopardise the delicate balance.

But at what price?

She had idiotically flung herself into something that had no future and when she should be doing all she could to redress the situation—when, in short, she should be pulling back—here she now was, even more deeply embedded and through no fault of her own.

The smell of him still clinging to her was a forceful reminder of how dangerous he could prove to be emotionally.

'If I dragged you into something you didn't court, then I apologise, but I acted on the spur of the moment.'

'That's all well and good, Giancarlo,' Caroline traded with spirit. 'But it's a *crazy* situation. Alberto believes we're *engaged*! What on earth is he going to do when he finds out that it was all a sham? Did you hear what he said about this giving him something to *carry on for*?'

'I heard,' Giancarlo admitted heavily. 'So the situation is not ideal. I realise it's a big favour, but I'm asking you to play along with it for a while.'

'Yes, but for how long?' A pretend engagement was a mocking, cruel reminder of what she truly wanted—which, shamefully, was a real engagement, excited plans for the future with the man she loved, *real* plans for a *real* future.

'How long is a piece of string? I'm not asking you to put your life on hold, but to just go with the flow for this window in time—after all, many engagements end in nothing.' Giancarlo propped himself up against the wall and glanced distractedly out towards breathtaking scenery, just snatches of it he could glimpse through the open shutters. 'In the meantime, anything could happen.' Why, he marvelled to himself, was this sitting so comfortably with him?

'You mean Alberto will come to accept that you're nothing like your mother, even though it's in your nature to have flings with women and then chuck them when you get bored?'

'Yet again your special talent for getting right to the heart of the matter,' Giancarlo gritted.

'But it's true, isn't it? Oh, I guess you could soft-soap him with something about us drifting apart, not really being suited to one another.'

'Breaking news—people *do* drift apart, people *do* end up in relationships only to find that they weren't suited to each other in the first place.'

'But you're different.' Caroline stubbornly stood

her ground. 'You don't give people a chance. Relationships with you never get to the point where you drift apart because they're rigged to explode long before then!'

'Is this your way of telling me that you have no intention of going along with this? That, although we've been sleeping together, you don't approve of me?'

'That's not what I'm saying!'

'Then explain. Because if you want me to tell Alberto the truth, that we're just having a bit of fun, then I will do that right now and we will both live with the consequences.'

And the consequences would be twofold: the fledgling relationship Giancarlo was building with his father would be damaged—not terminally, although Giancarlo could very well predetermine an outcome he might gloomily predict. And, of course, Alberto would be disappointed in her as well.

'I feel boxed in,' Caroline confessed. 'But I guess it won't be for long.' Would she have been able to sail through the pretence if her heart hadn't been at stake? She would have thought so, but if she felt vulnerable then it was something she would have to put up with, and who else was to blame if not herself? Had she ever thought that what she had with Giancarlo qualified for a happy-ever-after ending? 'I feel awful about deceiving your father, though.'

'Everyone deserves the truth, but sometimes a little white lie is a lot less harmful.'

'But it's not really *little*, is it?'

Giancarlo maintained a steady silence. It was beginning to dawn on him that he didn't know her as well as he had imagined. Or maybe he had arrogantly assumed that their very satisfying physical relationship would have guaranteed her willingness to fall in with what he wanted.

'Nor is it really a lie,' he pointed out softly. 'What we have *is* more than just a bit of fun.'

With all her heart, Caroline wanted to believe him, but caution allied with a keen sense of self-preservation prevented her from exploring that tantalising observation. How much *more* than just a bit of fun? she wanted to ask. How much did he *really* feel for her? Enough to one day love her?

She felt hopelessly vulnerable just thinking like that; she felt as though he might be able to see straight into her head and pluck out her most

shameful, private thoughts and desires. She wondered whether he had not dangled that provoca-
tive statement to win her over. Giancarlo would
not be averse to a little healthy manipulation if he
thought it might suit his own ends. But he needn't
have bothered trying to butter her up, she thought
gloomily. There was no way that she could ever
conceive of jeopardising what had been a truly
remarkable turnaround between father and son.
She would have had to be downright heartless to
have done so.

'Okay,' she agreed reluctantly. 'But not for long,
Giancarlo.'

Lush lashes lowered over his eyes, shielding his
expression. 'No,' he murmured. 'We'll take it one
day at a time.'

CHAPTER EIGHT

CAROLINE wished desperately that this new and artificial dimension to their relationship would somehow wake her up to the fact that they weren't an item. A week ago, when they had launched themselves into this charade, she had tried to get her brain to overrule her rebellious heart and pull back from Giancarlo, but within hours of Alberto's crazy misconceptions all her plans had nosedived in the face of one unavoidable truth.

They were supposedly a couple, madly in love, with the clamour of wedding bells chiming madly in the distance, so gestures of open physical affection were suddenly *de rigeur.* Giancarlo seemed to fling himself into the role of besotted lover with an enthusiasm that struck her as beyond the call of duty.

'How on earth are we ever going to find the right time to break it to your father that we're *drifting apart,* when you keep touching me every time we're together? We're not giving the impression of two people who have made a terrible mistake!' she had cried, three days previously after a lazy day spent by his infinity pool. Those slight brushes against her, the way he had held her in the water under Alberto's watchful gaze, were just brilliant at breaking down all her miserable defences. In fact, she was fast realising that she had no defences left. Now and again, she reminded herself to mutter something pointed to Giancarlo under her breath, but she was slowly succumbing to the myth they had fabricated around themselves.

'One day at a time,' he had reminded her gently.

He was beautifully, staggeringly, wonderfully irresistible and, although she *knew* that it was all a fiction which would of course backfire and injure her, she was lulled with each passing hour deeper and deeper into a feeling of treacherous happiness.

Alberto made no mention of their sleeping arrangements. Ideally, Caroline knew that she and Giancarlo should no longer be sleeping together. Ideally, she should be putting him at a distance, and sleeping with him was just the opposite of that. But every time that little voice of reason popped up, another more strident voice would take charge of the proceedings and tell her that she no longer had anything left to lose. She was with Giancarlo on borrowed time so why not just enjoy herself?

Besides, whether he was aware of it or not, he was burying all her noble intentions with his humour, his intelligence, his charm. Instead of feeling angry with him for putting her in an un-enviable position with Alberto, she felt increas-ingly more vulnerable. With Alberto and Tessa, they explored the coastline, stopping to have lunch at any one of the little towns that clung valiantly to the hilltop from which they could overlook the limpid blue sea. Giancarlo was relaxed and lazily, heart-stoppingly attentive. Just walking hand in hand with him made her toes curl and her heart beat faster.

And now they were going to Milan for three days. The last time she had gone to Milan, her purpose for the visit had been entirely different. Today she was going because Giancarlo had stuff to do that needed his physical presence.

'I think I should stay behind,' she had suggested

weakly, watching while he had unbuttoned her top and vaguely thinking that her protestations were getting weaker with every button undone.

'You're my beloved fiancée.' Giancarlo had given her a slashing smile that brooked no argument. 'You should *want* to see where I work and where I live.'

'Your *pretend* fiancée.'

'Let's not get embroiled in semantics.'

By which time he had completely undone her blouse, rendering her instantly defenceless as he stared with brazen hunger at her abundant, braless breasts. As he closed his eyes, spread his hands over her shoulders and took one pouting nipple into his mouth, she completely forgot what she had been saying.

By the time they made it to Milan, Caroline had had ample opportunity to see Giancarlo in work mode. They had taken the train, because Giancarlo found it more relaxing, and also because he wanted the undisturbed time to focus and prepare for the series of meetings awaiting him in Milan. An entire first-class carriage had been reserved for them and they were waited on with the reverential subservience reserved for the very wealthy and the very powerful.

This was no longer the Giancarlo who wore low-slung shorts and loafers without socks and laughed when she tried to keep up with him in the swimming pool. This was a completely different Giancarlo, as evidenced in his smart suit, a charcoal-grey, pin-striped, hand-tailored affair, the jacket of which he had tossed on one of the seats. In front of his laptop computer—frowning as he scrolled down pages and pages of reports; engaging in conference calls which he conducted in a mixture of French, English and Italian, moving fluently between the languages as he spoke with one person then another—he was a different person.

Caroline attempted to appreciate the passing scenery but time and again her eyes were drawn back to him, fascinated at this aspect to the man she loved.

'I'm just going to get in your way,' she said at one point, and he looked up at her with a slow smile.

'I hope so. Especially at night. In my bed. I definitely want you in my way then.'

It was late by the time they made it to Milan. Meetings would start in the morning, which was fine, because there was so much she wanted to see in the city that she had not found the time for on her previous visit. While Giancarlo worked, she would explore the city, and she had brought a number of guide books with her for that purpose.

Right now, as they were ushered into the chauffeur-driven car waiting for them at the station, she was just keen to see where he actually lived.

After the splendid seclusion of his villa on the coast and the peaceful tranquility of the view over the sea, the hectic frenzy of Milan, tourists and workers peopling the streets and pavements like ants on a mission, was an assault on all the senses. But it was temporary, for his apartment was in one of the small winding streets with its stunning eighteenth-century paving with a view of elegant gardens. Caroline didn't need an estate agent to tell her that she was in one of the most prestigious postcodes in the city.

The building in front of which the air-conditioned car finally stopped was the last word in elegance. A historic palace, it had clearly been converted into apartments for the ultra-wealthy and was accessed via wrought-iron gates, as intricate as lace, which led into a beautiful courtyard.

She openly goggled as Giancarlo led the way through the courtyard into the ancient building and up to his penthouse which straddled the top two floors.

He barely seemed to notice the unparalleled, secluded luxury of his surroundings. In a vibrant city, the financial beating heart of Italy, this was an oasis.

His apartment was not at all what she had expected. Where his villa on the coast was cool and airy, with louvred windows and voile curtains that let the breeze in but kept the ferocity of the sun out, this was all dark, gleaming wooden floors, rich drapes, exquisite furniture and deep, vibrant Persian rugs.

'This is amazing,' she breathed, standing still in one spot and slowly turning round in a circle so that she could take in the full entirety of the vast room into which she had been ushered.

Much more dramatically than ever before, she was struck by the huge, gaping chasm between them. Yes, they were lovers, and yes, he enjoyed her, lusted after her, desired her, couldn't keep his hands off her, but really and truly they inhabited two completely different worlds. Her parents' house was a tiny box compared to this apartment. In fact, the entire ground floor could probably have slotted neatly into the entrance hall in which she was now standing.

'I'm glad you approve.' He moved to stand behind her and wrapped his arms around her, burying his face in her long hair, breathing in the clean smell of her shampoo. She was wearing a flimsy cotton dress, with thin spaghetti straps and he slowly pulled these down, and from behind began unfastening the tiny pearl poppers. She wasn't wearing a bra and he liked that. He had long disbanded any notion of her in fine lingerie. If he had his way, she would never wear any at all.

'Show me the rest of the apartment.' She began doing up the poppers he had undone but it was a wasted mission because as fast as she buttoned them up he proceeded to unbutton them all over again.

'I'm hungry for you. I've had a long train trip with far too many people hovering in the background, making it impossible for me to touch you.'

Caroline laughed with the familiar pleasure of hearing him say things like that, things that made her feel womanly, desirable, heady and powerful all at the same time.

'Why is sex so important to you?' she murmured with a catch in her voice as he began playing with her breasts, his big body behind her so that she could lean against him, as weak as a kitten as his fingers teased the tips of her nipples into tight little buds.

'Why do you always initiate deep and meaningful conversations when you know that talking is the last thing on my mind?' But he chuckled softly. 'I should be making inroads into my reports but I can't stop wanting you for long enough,' he murmured roughly.

'I'm not sure that's a good thing.' She had arched back and was breathing quickly and unsteadily, eyes fluttering closed as he rolled the sensitised tips of her nipples between gentle fingers.

'I think it's a *very* good thing. Would you like to see my bedroom?'

'I'd like to see the *whole* apartment, Giancarlo.'

He gave an elaborate sigh and released her with grudging reluctance. He had long abandoned the urge to get to the bottom of her appeal. He just knew that, the second he was in her presence, he couldn't seem to keep his hands off her. Hell, even when she wasn't around she somehow still managed to infiltrate his brain so that images of her were never very far away. It was one reason he hadn't hesitated to ask her to accompany him to Milan. He just couldn't quite conceive not having her there when he wanted her. He also couldn't believe how much time he had taken off work. He wondered whether his body had finally caught up with him after years of being chained to the work place.

'Okay.' He stepped back, watched with his hands in his pockets as she primly and regrettably did up all those annoying little pearl buttons that ran the length of her dress. 'Guided tour of the apartment.'

While he was inclined to hurry over the details, Caroline took her time, stopping to admire every small fixture; gasping at the open fireplace in the sitting-room; stroking the soft velvet of the deep burgundy drapes; marvelling at the cunning way the modern appliances in the kitchen sat so comfortably alongside the old hand-painted Italian tiles on the wall and the exquisite kitchen table with its mosaic border and age-worn surface.

His office, likewise, was of the highest specification, geared for a man who was connected to the rest of the working world twenty-four-seven. Yet the desk that dominated the room looked to be centuries old and on the built-in mahogany shelves spanning two of the walls, first-edition books on the history of Italy nestled against law manuals and hardbacks on corporate tax.

Up a small series of squat stairs, four enormous bedrooms shared the upstairs space with a sitting-room in which resided the only television in the apartment.

'Not that I use it much,' Giancarlo commented when he saw her looking at the plasma screen. 'Business news. That's about it.'

'Oh, you're so boring, Giancarlo. *Business news!* Don't you get enough business in your daily life without having to spend your leisure time watching more of it on the telly?'

Giancarlo threw back his head and laughed, looking at her with rich appreciation. 'I don't think anyone's ever called me *boring* before. You're good for me, do you know that?'

'Like a tonic, you mean?' She smiled. 'Well, I don't think anyone has ever told me that before.'

'Come into my bedroom,' he urged her along, restlessly waiting as she poked her head into all of the bedrooms and emitted little cries of delight at something or other, details which he barely noticed from one day to the next. Yes, the tapestry on that wall behind that bed was certainly vibrant in colour; of course that tiffany lamp was beautiful and, sure, those narrow strips of stained glass on either side of the window were amazing. He couldn't wait to get her to his bedroom. He was tormented at the prospect of touching her and feeling her smooth, soft, rounded body under his hands. His loss of self-control whenever she was around still managed to astound him.

'Your mother must have been really proud of you, Giancarlo, to have seen you scale these heights.'

'Mercenary as I now discover she really was?' He shot her a crooked smile and Caroline frowned. 'How long have you been storing up that question?'

'You're so contained and I didn't want to bring up an uncomfortable subject. Not when things have been going so well between you and Alberto, yet I can't help but think that you must be upset at finding out that things weren't as you thought.'

'Less than I might have imagined,' Giancarlo confessed, linking his fingers with hers and leading her away from where she was heading towards one of the windows through which she would certainly exclaim at the view outside. It was one which still managed to impress him, and he was accustomed to it. 'Hell, I should be livid at the fact that my mother rewrote the past and determined my future to suit the rules of her own game, but...'

But he wasn't, because Caroline seemed to cushion him, seemed to be the soothing hand that was making acceptance easier. She was the softly spoken voice that blurred the edges of a bitterness that failed to surface. It made his head spin when he thought about it.

'I'm old enough to be able to put things in perspective. When I was younger, I wasn't. My youth helped determine my hardline attitude to my father but now that I'm older I see that my mother never really grew up. In a funny way, I think she would have been happier if Alberto really had been the guy she portrayed him as being. She would have found toughness easier to handle than understanding. He actually kept supporting her even when she had shown him that she was irresponsible with money, and would have taken everything and thrown it all away had Alberto not had the good sense to lock most of it up. He had bank statements going back for well over a decade.'

He hesitated. 'Three years after we left, she made an attempt to get back with my father. He turned her down. I think that was when she decided that she could punish him by making sure he never saw me.'

'How awful.' Caroline's eyes stung with sympathy but Giancarlo gave an expressive, philosophical shrug.

'It's in the past, and don't feel sorry for me. Adriana might have had dubious motivations for her behaviour—she certainly did her best to screw up whatever relationship I might have had with my father—but she could also be great fun and something of an adventurer. It wasn't all bad. She just spoke without thinking, acted without foreseeing consequences and was a little too gullible when it came to the opposite sex. In the end she was as much a victim of her own bitterness as I was.'

They had reached his bedroom and he pushed open the door, gazing with boyish satisfaction at her look of pleasure as she tentatively stepped into the vast space.

One wall was entirely dominated by a massive arched window that offered a bird's-eye view of Milan. She walked towards it, looked out and then turned round to find him watching her with a smile.

'I know you think I'm gauche.' She blushed.

'Don't worry about it. I happen to like that.'

'Everything's so *grand* in this apartment.'

'I know. I never thought it would be my style. Maybe I find it restful, considering the remainder of my life is so hectic.' He walked slowly towards her and Caroline felt that small frisson of anticipated pleasure as he held her gaze. 'It's easy to forget that the rest of the world exists outside this apartment.' He curved one hand around her waist. With the other, he unhooked the heavy taupe drape from a cord, instantly shrouding the room in semi-darkness.

He gathered her into his arms and they made love slowly. He lingered on her body, drawing every last breath of pleasure out of her, and in turn she lingered over his so that the chocolate-brown sheets and covers on the bed became twisted under their bodies as they repositioned themselves to enjoy one another.

It was dark by the time they eventually surfaced. A single phone call ensured that food was brought to them so that they could eat in the apartment, although Caroline was laughingly appalled at the fact that his fridge was bare of all but the essentials.

Despite the opulence of the decor, this was strictly a bachelor's apartment. Lazing around barefoot in one of his tee shirts, she teased him about his craziness in stocking the finest cheeses in his fridge but lacking eggs; having the best wines and yet no milk; and she pointed to all the shiny, gleaming gadgets and made him list which he was capable of using and which were never touched.

She let herself enjoy the seductive domesticity of being in his space. After a delicious dinner, they washed the dishes together—because he frankly hadn't a clue how to operate the dish-washer—and then she curled into him on the huge sofa in the sitting-room, reading while he flicked through papers with his arm lazily around her.

It all felt so right that it was easy to push away the notion that her love was making a nonsense of her pride and her common sense.

'Wake me up before you leave in the morning,' she made him promise, turning to him in bed and sliding her body against his. She had always covered herself from head to toe whenever she had gone to bed but he had changed all that. Now she slept naked and she loved the feel of his hard body against hers. When she covered his thigh with hers, the pleasure was almost unbearable.

Giancarlo grinned and kissed the corner of her mouth as she tried to disguise a delicate yawn.

'Have I worn you out?'

'You're insatiable, Giancarlo.'

'Only for you, *mi amore*, only for you.'

Caroline fell asleep clutching those words to herself, safeguarding them so that she could pull them out later and examine them for content and meaning.

When she next opened her eyes, it was to bright

sunshine trying to force its way through the thick drapes. Next to her the bed was empty and a sleepy examination of the apartment revealed that Giancarlo had left. She wondered what time he had gone, and tried to squash the niggling fear that he might be going off her. Was he? Or was she reading too much in the fact that he had left without saying goodbye? It was hardly nine yet. In the kitchen, prominently displayed on the granite counter, were six eggs, a loaf of bread, some milk and a note informing her that he could be as twenty-first-century as any other man when it came to stocking his larder.

Caroline smiled. It was hardly an outpouring of emotion, but there was something weirdly pleasing about that admission, an admission of change whether he saw it as such or not. She made herself some toast and scrambled eggs, finally headed out with her guide books at a little after ten and, pleasantly exhausted after several hours doing all those touristy things she had missed out on first time around, returned with the warming expectation of seeing him later that evening.

'I might be late,' he had warned her the night before. 'But no later than eight-thirty.'

It gave her oodles of time to have a long, luxurious bath and then to inspect herself in the mirror in the new outfit she had bought that morning. It was a short flared skirt that felt lovely and silky against her bare skin and a matching vest with three tiny buttons down the front. When she left the buttons undone, as she now did, her cleavage was exposed and she knew that without a bra he would be able to see the swing of her heavy breasts and the outline of her nipples against the thin fabric.

Of course she would never go bra-less in public, not in something as thin and flimsy as this top was, but she imagined the flare in his dark eyes when he saw her and felt a lovely shiver of anticipation.

With at least another couple of hours to go, she was thrilled to hear the doorbell ring.

She was smiling as she pulled open the door. Very quickly, her smile disappeared and confusion took over.

'Who are you?'

The towering, leggy blonde with hair falling in a straight sheet to her waist spoke before Caroline had time to marshal her scattered thoughts.

'What are you doing here? Does Giancarlo know that you're here? Are you the maid? Because, if you are, then your dress code is inappropriate. Let me in. Immediately.'

She pushed back the door and Caroline stepped aside in complete bewilderment. She hadn't had time to get a single word in, and now the impossibly beautiful blonde in the elegant short silk shift with the designer bag and the high, high heels that elevated her to over six feet, was in the apartment and staring around her through narrowed, suspicious eyes which finally came to rest once more on Caroline's red, flustered face.

'So.' The blonde folded her arms and looked at Caroline imperiously. 'Explain!'

'Who *are* you?' She had to crane her neck upwards to meet the other woman's eyes. 'Giancarlo didn't tell me that he was expecting anyone.'

'*Giancarlo?* Since when is the maid on first-name terms with her employer? Wait until he hears about this.'

'I'm *not* the maid. I'm…I'm…' There was no way that he would want her to say anything along the lines of 'fiancée', not when it was a relationship fabricated for Alberto's benefit, not when it meant nothing. 'We're…involved.'

The blonde's mouth curled into a smile that got wider and wider until she was laughing with genuine incredulity, while Caroline stood frozen to the spot. Her brain seemed to have shifted down several gears and was in danger of stalling completely. Next to such stupendous beauty, she felt like a complete fool.

'You have *got* to be joking!'

'I'm not, actually.' Caroline pulled herself up to her unimpressive height of a little over five-three. 'We've been seeing each other for a few weeks now.'

'He'd never go out with someone like you,' the blonde said in an exaggeratedly patient voice, the voice of someone trying to convey the obvious to a deluded lunatic.

'Sorry?' Caroline uttered huskily.

'I'm Lucia. Giancarlo and I were an item before I broke it off a few months ago. Pressure of work. I'm a model, by the way. I hate to tell you this, but *I'm* the sort of woman Giancarlo dates.'

There was an appreciable pause during which Caroline deduced that she was to duly pay heed,

take note and join the dots: Giancarlo dated mod-
els. He liked them long, leggy and blonde; short,
round and brunette was not to his liking. She
wished, uncharitably, that she was wearing an engagement ring, a large diamond cluster which she
could thrust into the blonde's smirking face, but
the trip to the jeweller's had not yet materialised
despite Alberto's gentle prodding.

'Look, tell him I called, would you?'

Caroline watched as Lucia—elegant name for
an elegant blonde—strutted towards the door.

'Tell him…' Lucia paused. Her cool blue eyes
swept over Caroline in a dismissive once-over.
'That he was right. Crazy hours flying all over the
world. Tell him that I've decided to take a rest for
a while, so he can reach me whenever he wants.'

'Reach you to do *what*?' She forced the question out, although her mouth felt like cotton wool.

'What do you think?' Lucia raised her eyebrows
knowingly. Despite her very blonde hair, her eyebrows were dark; a stunning contrast. 'Look, you
must think I'm a bitch for saying this, but I'll say it
anyway because it's for your own good. Giancarlo
might be having a little fun with you because he's
broken up about me, but that's all you are and it's

not going to last. Do yourself a favour and get out while you can. *Ciao*, darling!'

Caroline remained where she was for a few minutes after Lucia had disappeared. Her brain felt sluggish. It was making connections and the process hurt.

This was Giancarlo's real life—beautiful women who suited his glamorous life. He had taken time out and had somehow ended up in bed with her and now she knew why. In extraordinary circumstances, he had behaved out of character, had fallen into bed with the sort of woman who under normal circumstances he would have overlooked, because she was the sort of woman he might employ as his maid.

Even more terrifying was the suspicion that she had just been *there*, a convenient link between himself and his father. She had bridged a gap that could have been torturously difficult to bridge, and by the way had leapt into bed with him as an added bonus. He had found himself in a win-win situation and, Giancarlo being Giancarlo, he had taken full advantage of the situation. The note she had found, which she had optimistically seen as the sign of someone learning to really share, now seemed casual and dismissive, a few scribbled lines paying lip service to someone who had made his life easier; a willing bed companion who gave him the privileges of a real relationship while conveniently having expectations of none.

Caroline hurt all over. She felt ridiculous in her stupid outfit and was angry and ashamed of having dressed for him. She was mortified at the ease with which she had allowed herself to be taken over body and soul until all her waking moments revolved around him. She had dared to think the impossible—that he would love her back.

She hurried to change. Off came the silly skirt and the even sillier top. She found that her hands were shaking as she rifled through her belongings, picking out a pair of jeans and a tee shirt. It was like stepping back into her old life and back into reality. She stuffed the new outfit—which only hours before had given her such pleasure as she had looked at her reflection in the changing room of the overpriced Italian boutique—into the front pocket of her suitcase which she usually kept for her shoes and dirty clothes.

She very much wanted to run away, but she made herself turn the telly on, and there she was when an hour and a half later she heard Giancarlo slot his key into the door.

She had a horrid image of herself in her silly outfit, scampering to the front door like a perfectly trained puppy greeting its master, and she forced herself to remain exactly where she was in front of the television until he walked into the sitting-room. As he strolled towards her, with that killer smile curving his mouth, he began loosening his tie and unbuttoning his shirt.

Bitter and disillusioned as she was, Caroline still couldn't contain her body's instinctive reaction, and she strove to quell the feverish race of her pulse and the familiar drag on her senses. She pulled up the image of the blonde and focused on that.

'You have no idea how much I've been looking forward to coming back…' Tie undone, he tossed it onto one of the sofas and walked towards her, leaning down over the chair into which she was huddled, his arms braced on either side, caging her in.

Caroline had trouble breathing.

'Really?'

'Really. You're very bad for me. Somehow trying to work out the logistics of due diligence is a lot less fun than thinking about you waiting for me back here.'

Like a faithful, mindless puppy.

'I left my chief in command at the meeting. The option of seeing you here, well, it wasn't a difficult choice.'

Seeing me here...in your bed...

'Food first? My man at the Capello can deliver within the hour.'

Because why would you take me out and cut into the time you can spend in bed with me? Before you get bored, because I'm nothing like the girls you want to date, girls who look good hanging on your arm... Long, leggy girls with waist-length blonde hair and exotic, sexy names like Lucia...

'You're not talking.' Giancarlo vaulted upright and strolled towards the closest chair, where he sat and then leaned forwards, his arms on his thighs. 'I'm sorry I couldn't go sightseeing with you today. Believe me, I would have loved to have shown you my city. Were you bored?'

Caroline unfroze and rediscovered the power of speech. 'I had a very nice time. I visited the

Duomo, the museum and I had a very nice lunch in one of the *piazzas*.'

'I'm guessing that there's a 'but' tacked on to that description of your *very nice* day with the *very nice* lunch?' Something was going on here. Giancarlo could feel it, although he was at a loss to explain it.

He had woken next to her at a ridiculously early hour and had paused to look at her perfectly contented face as she slept on her side, one arm flung up, her hands balled into fists, the way a baby would sleep. She had looked incredibly young, and incredibly tempting. He had had to resist the urge to wake her at the ungodly hour of five-thirty to make love. Instead he had taken a cold shower and had spent most of the day counting down to when he would walk through the front door. Never before could he remember having such a craving to return to his apartment. 'Wherever he laid his hat' had never been his definition of home.

He frowned as a sudden thought occurred to him.

'Did something happen today?' he asked slowly. 'I take no responsibility for my fellow Italians, but it's not unheard of for some of them to be forward with tourists. Did you get into some bother while you were sightseeing? Someone follow you? Made a nuisance of himself?' He could feel himself getting hot under the collar, and he clenched and unclenched his fists at the distasteful thought of someone pestering her, making her day out a misery.

'Something *did* happen,' Caroline said quietly, her eyes sliding away from him because even the sight of him was enough to scramble her brains. 'But nothing like what you're saying. I didn't get into any bother when I was out. And, by the way, even if someone *had* made a nuisance of himself I'm not a complete idiot. I would have been able to handle the situation.'

'What, then?'

'I had a visit.' This time she rested her eyes steadily on his beautiful face. A person could drown in those dark, fathomless eyes, she thought. Hadn't *she*?

'A visit *here*?'

Caroline nodded. 'Tall. Leggy. Blonde. You might know who I mean. Her name was Lucia.'

CHAPTER NINE

GIANCARLO stilled.

'Lucia was *here*?' he asked tightly. The hard lines of his face reflected his displeasure. Lucia Fontana was history, one of his exes who had taken their break-up with a lot less grace than most. She was a supermodel at the height of her career, accustomed to men lusting after her, paying homage to her beauty, contriving to be in her presence. She was also, in varying degrees, annoying, superficial, vain, self-centred and lacking in anything that could be loosely termed *intelligence*. She had met him at a business function, an art exhibition which had been attended by the glitterati, and she had pursued him. His mistake had been lazily to go along for the ride. 'What the hell was she doing here?'

'Not expecting to find *me*,' Caroline imparted tonelessly. She toyed with the idea of telling him that the blonde had, at first, assumed that she was the maid, the hired help dressed inappropriately for the job of scrubbing floors and cleaning the toilets. She decided to keep that mortifying titbit to herself.

'I apologise for that. Don't worry. It won't happen again.'

Caroline shrugged. Did he expect her to be grateful for that heartening promise, just because she happened to be the flavour of the month, locked in a situation which neither of them could ever have foreseen? She felt an uncharacteristic temptation to snort with disgust.

'I expect there's probably a whole barrel-load of them lurking in the woodwork, waiting to crawl out at any minute.'

'What the hell are you talking about?'

'Women. Exes. Glamorous supermodels you threw over or, in the case of this one, a glamorous supermodel who threw *you* over.'

'Lucia? Did she tell you that she left me?' Giancarlo felt a surge of white-hot rage rip through him. He knew that he had badly dented her ego when he had dumped her, but the thought of her coming to his apartment and lying through her pearly-white teeth made him see red.

'Well, I guess it must have been difficult for her to conduct a relationship with someone when she was travelling all over the place, but she said that she's back now and you can contact her whenever you want. Pick up where you left off.'

No; he was not going to start explaining himself. No way. That was a road he had never been down and he wasn't about to go down it now. It just wasn't in his nature to justify his behaviour, not that he had anything *to* justify!

'And this is what you'll be expecting me to do, is it?' he asked coolly.

Caroline felt her heart breaking in two. She hadn't realised how much she had longed to hear him deny everything the other woman had said. His silence on the subject was telling. Okay, so maybe he wasn't going to race over to Lucia's apartment and fling himself at her feet, but surely if the other woman had been lying he would have denied her story?

'You've gone into a mood because, despite everything, you don't trust me.'

'I'm not in a mood!'

'That's not what my eyes are telling me. Lucia and I were finished months ago.'

'But did you end it or did *she*?'

'What difference does it make? You either trust me or you don't.'

'Why should I trust you, Giancarlo?' She had been determined not to lose her rag, but looking at his proud, aristocratic face she wanted to slap him. Her own crazy love for him, her stupidity in thinking that what they had meant something, rose up like bile to her throat.

'You wouldn't have looked twice at someone like me if we'd met under more normal circumstances, would you?'

'I refuse to get embroiled in a hypothetical discussion of what might or might not have happened. We met and you've had more than ample proof of how attracted I am to you.'

'But I'm not *your type*. I guess I knew that all along—deep down. But your girlfriend made it very clear that—'

'Lucia is *not* my girlfriend. Okay, if it means that much to you to know what happened between us, I'll tell you! I went out with the woman and it turned out to be a mistake. There's only room for one person in Lucia's life and that's Lucia. She's an airhead who can only talk about herself. No mirror is safe when she's around, and aside from that she's got a vicious tongue.'

'But she's beautiful.' Caroline found that she no longer cared about who had done the breaking up. What did it matter? Dig deep and the simple fact was that Lucia was more his type than *she* was. He liked them transient; playthings that wouldn't take up too much of his valuable time and wouldn't make demands of him.

'I dumped her and she took it badly.' He hadn't meant to explain himself but in the end he had been unable *not* to.

'Well, it doesn't matter.'

'It clearly does or you wouldn't be making such a big deal of this.'

Caroline thought that what was nothing to him was a very big deal for her, except there was no way that he would understand that because he hadn't dug himself into the same hole that she had. Every sign of hurt would be just another indication to him of how deeply embedded she had become in their so-called relationship.

What would he do if he discovered that she was in love with him? Laugh out loud? Run a mile? Both? She was determined that he wouldn't find out. At least then she would be able to extract herself with some measure of dignity instead of proving Lucia right, proving that she had made the fatal error of thinking that she meant more to Giancarlo than she did.

Unable to contain her agitation, she stood up and paced restlessly towards the window, peering outside in search of inspiration, then she perched on the broad ledge so that she was sitting on her hands. That way, they kept still.

'I was embarrassed,' Caroline told him. She swallowed back the tears of self-pity that were vying for prevalence over her self-control. 'I hadn't expected to open the door to one of your ex-girlfriends, although it's not your fault that she showed up here. I realise that. She said some pretty hurtful things and that's not your fault either.'

Considering that he was being exonerated of all blame from the sound of it, Giancarlo was disturbed to find that he didn't feel any better. And he didn't like the remote expression on her face. He preferred it when she had been angry, shouting at him, backing him into a corner.

'It *did* make me think, though, that what we're doing is… Well, we need to stop it.'

'Work that one through for me. One stupid woman turns up uninvited on my doorstep and suddenly you've decided that what we have is a bad idea? We're adults, Caroline. We're attracted to one another.'

'We're deceiving an old man into thinking that this is something that it isn't, and I should have listened to my conscience from the start. It's not just about having fun, never mind the consequences.'

Giancarlo flushed darkly, for once lost for words. If Lucia had been in the room, he would have throttled her. It was unbelievable just how wrong the evening had gone. The worst of it was that he could feel Caroline slipping away from him and there was nothing he could do about it.

'The fact is, that woman was right. I'm not your type.' She couldn't help herself. She left a pause, a heartbeat of silence, something he could fill with a denial. 'You're not my type. We've been having fun, and in the process leading Alberto into thinking that there's more to what we have than there actually is.'

'It's crazy to come back to the hoary subject of

type.' Even to his own ears he sounded like a man on the back foot, but any talk about the value of 'having fun', which seemed to have become dirty words, would land him even further in the quagmire. He raked frustrated fingers through his hair and glowered at her.

'Maybe if Alberto wasn't involved things might have been a bit different.'

'Isn't it a bit late in the day to start taking the moral high ground?'

'It's never too late in the day to do the right thing.'

'And a woman who meant nothing to me, who was an albatross around my neck after the first week of seeing her, has brought you to this conclusion?'

'I've woken up.' She felt as though she was swallowing glass and her nerves went into frantic overdrive as he stood up to walk towards her.

Everything about him was achingly familiar, from the smell of him to the supple economy of his movements. Her imagination only had to travel a short distance to picture the feel of his muscular arms under his shirt.

She half-turned but her breathing was fast. More

than anything else in the world, she didn't want him to touch her.

'I know it's late, but I really think I'd like to get back to the villa.'

'This is crazy!'

'I need to be—'

'Away from me? Because if you stay too close you're scared that your body might take over?' He muttered a low oath in the face of her continuing silence.

'I don't mind heading back tonight.'

'Forget it! You can leave in the morning, and I'll make sure that I'm not under your feet tonight. I'll instruct my driver to be here for you at nine. My private helicopter will take you back to the villa.' He turned away and began striding towards the bedroom. After a second's hesitation, Caroline followed him, galvanised into action and now terrified of the void opening up at her feet, even though she knew that there was no working her way around it.

'I know you're concerned about Alberto getting the wrong impression of you.'

She hovered by the door, desperate to maintain contact, although she knew that she had lost him. He was turning away, stripping off his shirt to hurl it on the antique chair that sat squarely under the window.

'I'll tell him that your meetings were so intensive that we thought it better for me to head back to the coast, to get out of the stifling heat in Milan.'

Giancarlo didn't answer. She found her feet taking her forwards until she was standing in front of him.

'Giancarlo, please. Don't be like this.'

He paused and looked at her with a shuttered expression. 'What do you want me to say, Caroline?'

She shrugged and stared mutely down at her feet.

'Where are you going to go? I mean, tonight? You said that you'll make sure that you aren't under my feet.' She placed one small hand on his arm and he looked down at it pointedly.

'If you want to touch, then you have to be prepared for the consequences.'

Caroline whipped her hand away and took a couple of unsteady steps back. He had said that before. Once. And back then, light-years ago, she had reached out and touched because she had wanted to fall into bed with him. Now she wanted to run as fast as she could away from him. How had she managed to breach the space between them? It was as if her body, in his presence, had a mind of its own and was drawn to him like a moth to a flame.

'This is your apartment. It's—it's silly for you to go somewhere else for the night,' she stammered.

'What are you suggesting? That I climb into bed next to you and we both go to sleep like chaste babes in the wood?'

'I could use one of the spare bedrooms.'

'I wouldn't trust me if I were you,' Giancarlo murmured, keen eyes watching her as she went a delicate shade of pink. 'You might just wake up to find me a little too close for comfort. Now, I'm going to have a shower. Do you want to continue this conversation in the bathroom?'

Her heart was still beating fast twenty minutes later when Giancarlo reappeared in his sitting-room, showered, changed and with a small overnight bag. He looked refreshed, calm and controlled. She, on the other hand, was perched on the edge of the sofa, her back erect, her hands primly resting on her knees. She looked at him warily.

'You do know,' he said, dropping his bag on one of the sprawling sofas and strolling towards the kitchen, where he proceeded to pour himself a drink, 'that I'll be heading back to the coast once this series of meetings is finished? So I need to know exactly what I'm going to be walking into.'

'Walking into?' She was riveted by the sight of him in a pair of faded jeans and a polo shirt in a similar colour, so different from the businessman who had walked through the door, and all over again she agonised as to whether she had made the right decision. Distressed and disconcerted by Lucia's appearance, had she overreacted? She loved Giancarlo! Had she blown whatever chance she had of somehow getting him to feel the way she felt? If they had continued seeing one another, would love eventually have replaced lust?

As soon as she started thinking like that, another scenario rushed up in her head. It was a scenario in which he became bored and disinterested, in which she became more and more needy and clingy. It was a scenario in which another Lucia clone came along, leggy, blonde and dim-witted, to lure him away from the challenge of someone who spoke too freely. He might find her frankness a novelty now, but it was not a trait he was used to—and did a leopard ever change its spots?

But the way he looked…

She swallowed and told herself just to *focus*.

'Now that you've seen the light, are you even planning on being there at the end of the week?'

'Of course I am! I told you that I'm prepared to go along with this for a short while longer, but we're going to have to show your father that we're drifting apart so that he won't be upset when we announce that it's over between us.'

'And any clues on how we should do that? Maybe we could stage a few arguments? Or you could play with the truth and tell him that you met one of my past girlfriends and you didn't like what you saw.'

Caroline thought of Lucia and she glanced hesitantly at Giancarlo. 'Were all your girlfriends like that?'

'Come again?'

'All your girlfriends, were they like Lucia?'

Giancarlo frowned, taken aback by the directness of the question and the gentle criticism he could detect underlying it.

'I know that Lucia might have annoyed you,'

she continued. 'But were they all like her? Have you ever been out with someone who wasn't a model? Or an actress? I mean, do you just go out with women because of the way they look?'

'I don't see the relevance of the question.' Nor could he explain how it was that a beautiful, intellectually unchallenging woman could be less of a distraction than the other way around. But that was indeed the case as far as he was concerned. He had not been programmed for distraction. Somewhere along the line, that hard-wiring had just failed.

'No. It's not relevant.' She looked away from him and he was savagely tempted to force himself into her line of vision and bring her back to his presence.

Instead, he slung his holdall over his shoulder and began heading towards the front door.

Caroline forced herself to stay put, but it was hard because her disobedient feet wanted to fly behind him and cling, keep him there with a few more questions. She wanted to ask him what he ever saw in her. She wasn't beautiful, so was there something else that attracted him? She wanted to prise anything favourable out of him but she bit back the words before they could tumble out of her mouth.

She thought of this so-called distancing that would have to take place and immediately missed the physical contact and the easy camaraderie. And the laughter. And everything else that had hooked her in.

She heard the quiet click of the front door shutting and the apartment suddenly felt very big and very, very empty.

With her mind in complete turmoil, she had no idea how she was ever going to get to sleep, but in actual fact she fell asleep easily and woke to thin grey light filtering through the crack in the heavy curtains. It took her a few seconds for the links in her mind to join up. Giancarlo wasn't there. The bed was empty. It hadn't been slept in. He was gone. For a few seconds more, she replayed events of the evening before. She was a spectator at a film, condemned to watch it even though she knew the ending and hated it.

The chauffeur was there promptly at nine, and Caroline was waiting for him, her bags packed. Right up until the last minute, she half-hoped to see Giancarlo appear. She guiltily allowed herself the fantasy of him appearing with a huge bouquet of flowers, red roses, full of apologies and possibly with a ring in a small box.

In the absence of any of that, she spent both the drive and the brief helicopter ride sickeningly scared at the very real possibility that he had left the apartment to seek solace in someone else's arms.

Would he do that? She didn't know. But then, how well did she know him, after all?

She had sworn that she had seen the complete man, but she had been living in a bubble. The Giancarlo she had known was not the same Giancarlo who dated supermodels because they were undemanding and because they looked good on his arm.

She felt a pang of agonising emptiness as finally, with both the drive and the helicopter ride behind her, the villa at last approached, cresting the top of the cliff like an imperious master ruling the waves beneath it.

What they had shared was over. She had been so busy dwelling on that that she had given scant thought as to what she would actually say to Alberto when she saw him.

Now, as she stepped out of the taxi which had taken her from the helipad close by to the house, her thoughts shifted into another gear.

They had as left the happy couple. How easy was it going to be to convince Alberto that in the space of only a few hours that had all begun un-ravelling?

As she frantically grappled with the prospect of yet more half-truths, and before she could slot the spare key which she had been given when they first arrived at the villa into the lock, the front door was pulled open and she was confronted with the sight of a fairly flabbergasted Alberto.

Caroline smiled weakly as he peered around her in search of Giancarlo.

'What's going on? Shouldn't you be in Milan on the roof terraces of the Duomo with the rest of the tourists, making a nuisance of yourself with your camera and your guide book and getting in the way of the locals?' He frowned keenly at her. 'Something you want to tell me?' He stood aside. 'I was just on my way out for a little stroll in the gardens, to take a breather from the harridan, but from the looks of it we need to talk…'

* * *

Giancarlo looked at his watch for the third time. He was battle-hardened when it came to meetings, but this particular one seemed to be dragging its feet. It was now nearly four in the afternoon and they had been at it since six-thirty that morning, a breakfast meeting where strong coffee had made sure all participants were raring to go. There was a hell of a lot to get through.

Unfortunately, his mind was almost entirely pre-occupied with the woman he had left the previous evening.

He scowled at the memory and distractedly began tapping his pen on the conference table until all eyes were focused on him in anticipation of something very important being said. This was just the sort of awestruck respect to which he had become accustomed over time and which he now found a little irritating. Didn't any of these people have minds of their own? Was there a single one present who would dare risk contradicting anything he had to say? Or did he just have to tap a pen inadvertently to have them gape at him and fall silent?

He pushed his papers aside and stood up. Several half-rose and then resumed their seats.

Having spent the day in the grip of indecision, with his mind caught up in the last conversation he'd had with Caroline, Giancarlo had now reached a decision, and was already beginning to regain some of his usual self-assured buoyancy.

Step one was to announce to the assembled crew that he would be leaving, which was met with varying degrees of shock and surprise. Giancarlo walking out of a meeting was unheard of.

'Roberto.' He looked at the youngest member of the team, a promising lad who had no fear of long hours. 'This is your big chance for centre stage. You're well filled-in on the details of this deal. I will be contactable on my mobile, but I'm trusting you can handle the technicalities. Naturally, nothing will proceed without my final say-so.'

Which made at least one person extremely happy.

Step two involved a call to his secretary. Within minutes he was ready for the trip back to the coast. The helicopter was available but Giancarlo chose instead the longer option of the train. He needed to think.

Once on the train he checked his mobile for messages, stashed his computer bag away, because the last thing he needed was the distraction of work, and then gazed out of the window as the scenery flashed past him in an ever-changing riot of colour.

He was feeling better and better about his decision to leave Milan. Halfway through his trip, he reached the decision that he would start being more proactive in training up people who could stand in for him. Yes, he had a solid, dependable and capable network of employees, but he was still far too much the figurehead of the company, the one they all turned to for direction. Hell, he hadn't had time out for years!

It was dark by the time he arrived at the villa, and as he stood in front of it he paused to look at its perfect positioning and exquisite architectural detail. As getaways went, it was one that had seldom been used. He had just never seemed to find the down time. Getaways had been things for other people.

He let himself in and headed straight for the breezy patio at the front of the house. He knew the routine. His father would be outside, enjoying the fresh air, which he claimed to find more invigorating than the stuffiness of the lakes.

'Must be the salt!' he had declared authoritatively on day one, and Giancarlo had laughed and asked for medical proof to back up that sweeping statement.

It was a minute or two before Alberto was alerted to Giancarlo's shadowy figure approaching, and a few more seconds for Caroline to realise that they were no longer alone.

They had not switched on the bank of outside lights, preferring instead the soothing calm of the evening sky as the colours of the day faded into greys, reds and purples before being extinguished by black.

'Giancarlo!' Caroline was the first to break the silence. She stood up, shocked to see him silhouetted in front of her, tall and even more dramatically commanding because he was backlit, making it impossible for her to clearly see his face.

'We weren't expecting you.' Alberto looked shrewdly between them and waved Caroline back down. 'No need to stand, my girl. You're not in the presence of royalty.'

'What are you doing here?'

'Since when do I need a reason to come to my own house?'

'I just thought that in the light of what's happened you would remain in Milan.'

'In the light of what's happened?'

'I've told your father everything, Giancarlo. There's no need to pretend any longer.'

A thick silence greeted this flat statement and it stretched on and on until Caroline could feel herself begin to perspire with nervous tension. She wished he would move out to the patio. Anything but stand there like a sentinel, watching them both with a stillness that sent a shiver through her.

Caroline glanced over to Alberto for some assistance and was relieved when he rose to the occasion.

'Of course, I was deeply upset by this turn of events,' Alberto said sadly. 'I'm an old man with health problems, and perhaps I placed undue pressure on the both of you to feign something just for the purpose of keeping me happy. If that was the case, son, then it was inexcusable.'

'Aren't you being a little over-dramatic, Alberto?' Giancarlo stepped out to the patio and shoved his hands in his pockets.

'There is nothing over-dramatic about admitting to being a misguided old fool, Giancarlo. I can only hope that my age and frailty excuse me.' He stood up and gripped the arm of the chair, steadying himself and flapping Caroline away when she rose to help him.

'I'm old, but I'm not dead yet,' he said with a return of his feisty spirit. 'Now I suppose you two should do some talking. Sort out arrangements. I believe you mentioned to me that you would be thinking of heading back to foreign shores, my girl?'

Caroline frantically tried to remember whether she had said any such thing. Had she? Perhaps she had voiced that thought out loud. It certainly hadn't been one playing on her mind. In fact, she hadn't really considered her next move at all, although now that the suggestion was out in the open didn't it make horrible sense? Why would she want to stick around when the guy who had broken her heart would always be there on the sidelines, popping in to see his father?

Besides, surely she had a life to lead?

'Er...'

'In fact, it might be appropriate for us to leave

the coast, come to think of it. Head back to the lakes. We wouldn't want to take advantage of your hospitality, given the circumstances.'

'Papa, please. Sit down.'

'And I could have sworn that you two had chemistry. Just goes to show what a hopeful fool I was.'

'We got along fine.' Caroline waded in before Alberto could really put his foot in it. She had confessed everything to her employer, including how she felt about his son. Those were details with which he had been sworn to secrecy. 'We… we… We're just… I'm sure we'll remain friends.'

Giancarlo threw her a ferocious scowl and she wilted. So, not even friendship. It had been an impractical suggestion, anyway. There was no way she could remain friends with him. It would always hurt far too much.

'I'll toddle off now. Tessa will probably be fretting. Damn woman thinks I'm going off the rails if I'm not in bed by ten.'

Mesmerised by Giancarlo's unforgiving figure, Caroline was only dimly aware of Alberto making his way towards the sitting-room by the kitchen, where Tessa was watching her favourite soap on the television. Alberto would join her. Caroline was convinced that he was becoming hooked on it even though he had always been the first to decry anything as lightweight as a soap opera.

'So,' Giancarlo drawled, slowly covering the space between them until he was standing right in front of her.

'I know I said I wouldn't say anything to Alberto, but I got here and it all just poured out. I'm sorry. He was okay with it. We underestimated him. I don't understand why you came back, Giancarlo.'

'Disappointed, are you?' he asked fiercely. He stepped away from her and walked towards the wooden railing to lean heavily against it and stare out at the glittering silver ocean below.

He turned round to face her.

'Just surprised. I thought you had so much to do in Milan.'

'And if I hadn't shown up here tonight, would you have disappeared back to England without saying a word?'

'I don't know,' Caroline confessed truthfully. She bowed her head and stared down at her feet.

'Well, at least that's more honest than the last lot of assurances you gave me—when you said that you'd say nothing to my father. I can't talk to you here. I keep expecting Alberto to pop out at any minute and join in the conversation.'

'What's there to talk about?'

'Walk with me on the beach. Please.'

'I'd rather not. Now that your father has no expectations of us getting married or anything of the sort, we need to put what we had behind us and move on.'

'Is that what you want?' Giancarlo asked roughly. 'If I recall, you said that, were it not for Alberto, you would consider us… Well, Alberto is now out of the picture.'

'There's more to it than that,' Caroline mumbled. The breeze lifted her hair, cooled her hot face. Beneath her, the sound of the waves crashing against rocks was as soothing as an orchestral beat, although she didn't feel in the least soothed.

'I need more than just a physical relationship, Giancarlo, and I suppose that was what I finally faced up to when your ex-girlfriend paid a visit to your apartment. She's reality. She's the life you lead. I was just a step out of time. When you decided, for whatever reason, to return to Lake Como to see your father, you were doing something totally out of the ordinary. I was just part and parcel of your time out. It was fun but I want more than to just be someone's temporary time-out girl.'

'Don't tell me we're not suited to one another. I can't accept that.'

'Because you just can't imagine someone turning you down? I believe you when you say that you dumped Lucia—and yet there she was, a woman who could snap her fingers and have anyone she wanted, ready to do whatever it took to get you back.'

'And now the boot's on the other foot,' Giancarlo said in a husky undertone. 'Now I've found out what it's like to be that person who is willing to do whatever it takes to get someone back.'

CHATPER TEN

'YOU'RE just saying that,' Caroline whispered tautly. 'You just can't bear the thought of someone walking away from you.'

'I don't care who walks away from me. I just can't bear the thought that that person would be *you*.'

Caroline didn't want to give house room to any hope. One false move and it would begin taking over, like a pernicious weed, suffocating all her common sense and noble intentions. And then where would she be?

'Look, let's go down to the beach. It's private there.'

Caroline thought that that was exactly what she was scared of. Too much privacy with Giancarlo had always proved to be a disaster. On the other hand, what had he meant when he'd said that he would do whatever it took to get her back? Had she misheard?

'Okay,' she agreed, dragging that one word out with a pointed show of reluctance, just in case he got it into his head that he might have the upper hand. 'But I want to get to bed early. In the morning I think it would be best all round for us to leave, return to the lakes, and then I can start thinking about heading back to the U.K.' Her mind instantly went blank and she felt a sense of vague panic.

'I've already been in Italy far too long!' she babbled on brightly. 'Mum's started asking when I plan to return. It's been a brilliant experience over here. I may not be incredibly fluent but I can hold my own now in Italian. I think it's going to be so much easier to get a really good job.'

'I'm not all that interested in your prospective CV.'

'I'm just saying that I have lots of stuff planned for when I return home and, now that Alberto is back on his feet and this silliness between us is over, there's no reason for me to stay on.'

'Do you really think that what we had could be termed *silly*?'

Caroline fell silent. When on a frustrated sigh Giancarlo began heading towards the lawns, to the side gate that opened onto a series of steps that had been carved into the hillside so that the cove beneath could be accessed, she followed him. It was dark, but the walk down was lit and the steps, in a graceful arch, were broad, shallow and easily manoeuvred thanks to iron railings on either side. She had no idea what the cove was like. The walk was a bit too challenging for Alberto and she had hesitated to go on her own. In Giancarlo's presence, her fear of open water was miraculously nonexistent. Without him around, she had been dubious at the prospect of the small beach on her own. What if the tide rushed up and took her away?

'The water is very shallow here,' Giancarlo said, reading her mind. 'And very calm.'

'I wasn't scared.'

He paused to turn around and look at her. 'No. Why would you be? I'm here.'

Her heart skipped a beat and she licked her lips nervously. Although it was after nine, it was still warm. In the distance, the sea beyond the protected cove glinted silver and black, constantly changing as the waves rose, fell, crashed against rocks and ebbed away. It was an atmosphere that was intimate and romantic but all she felt was trepidation and an incredible sadness that her last memories of Giancarlo would probably be of him right here, on his own private beach. Whatever he said about doing whatever it took, she would know what he meant: he didn't want to lose.

The cove was small and private. Giancarlo slipped off his shoes and he felt the sand under his feet with remembered delight. Then he walked to the water's edge and looked out to the black, barely visible horizon.

Behind him, Caroline was as still as the night. In fact, he could hardly hear her breathing. What was she talking about, leaving the country, returning to the U.K.? Uncertainty made him unusually hesitant. She had confessed everything to Alberto. For him, that said it all. He turned round to see her perched on a flat slab of rock, her knees drawn up, her arms wrapped around herself. She was staring out to sea but as he walked towards her she looked up at him warily.

'I don't want you to leave,' he said roughly, staring down at her. 'I came back here because I had to see you. I couldn't concentrate. Hell, that's never happened to me before.'

'I'm sorry.'

He sat next to her on the sand. 'Is that all you have to say? That you're sorry? What about the bit where I told you that I don't want you to leave?'

'Why don't you? Want me to leave, that is?'

'Isn't it obvious?'

'No. It's not.' Caroline shifted her gaze back to the inky sea. 'This is all about you being attracted to me,' she said in a low, even voice. 'I don't suppose you expected that to happen when you first came to see your father. In fact, I don't suppose you expected lots of things to happen.'

'If by that you mean that I didn't expect to reconcile with Alberto, then you're right.'

'I'm just part of an unexpected chain of events.'

'I have no idea what you're talking about.'

'That's the problem.' Caroline sighed. 'You don't know what I'm talking about.'

'Then why don't you enlighten me?'

Caroline wondered how she could phrase her deeply held fear that she had been no more than a novelty. How many times, as they had laughed and made love and laughed again, had he marvelled at the feeling of having taken time out of his ordinary life? Like someone going on holiday for the first time, he had picked her up and enjoyed a holiday romance with her, but had he ever mentioned anything permanent? Had he ever made plans for a future? Now that she had found the strength to walk away from him, he had come dashing back because she hadn't quite outstayed her welcome. But she would.

'I feel that my life's been on hold and now it's time for me to move on,' she said in a low voice. 'I never really meant to stay for this length of time in Italy in the first place, but Alberto and I got along so well together, and then when he fell ill I didn't want to leave him to on his own.'

'What does that have to do with us?' A cold chill was settling in the pit of his stomach. This had all the signs of a Dear John letter and he didn't like it. He refused to accept it.

'I don't want to just hang around here, living with Alberto, waiting for the occasional weekend when you decide to come down to visit until you get sick of me and go back to the sort of life you've always led.'

'What if I don't want to go back to the life I've always led?'

'What are you saying?'

'Maybe I've realised that the life I've always led isn't all that it's cracked up to be.'

Caroline gave him a smile of genuine amusement. 'So you've decided that you'll take to the lakes and become a sailing instructor?'

'You're so perfect for me. You never take me seriously.'

On the contrary, Caroline thought that she took him *far* too seriously.

'You swore to me that you weren't going to say a word to my father.'

How did they get back to this place? Caroline frowned her puzzlement but then she gave an imperceptible shrug. 'I hadn't planned to,' she confessed truthfully. 'But Alberto was at the front door when I got back. I think if I'd had time to get my thoughts in order—I don't know… But he opened the door to me and I took one look at him and I just knew that I couldn't carry on with the deception. He deserved the truth. It doesn't matter now, anyway.'

'It matters to me. I came here to try and persuade you that I didn't want us to break up. We're good for one another.'

For that, Caroline read 'we're good in bed together'. She looked at him sceptically.

'You don't believe me.'

'I believe that you've had a good time with me, and maybe you'd like the good time to continue a little bit longer, but it's crazy to confuse that with something else.'

'Something else like what?' he asked swiftly and Caroline was suddenly hot and flustered.

'Like a reason for not breaking up,' she muttered. 'Like a reason for trying to persuade me to stay on in Italy when I'm long overdue for my return trip. Like a reason for persuading me to think that it's okay to put my life on hold because we're good in bed together.'

'And let's just say that I want you in my life for longer than a few weeks? Or a few months? Or a few years? Let's just say that I want you in my life for ever?'

Caroline was so shocked that she held her breath and stared at him wide-eyed and unblinking.

'You're not the marrying sort. You don't even like women getting their feet through your front door.'

'You have an annoying habit of quoting me back

to myself.' But he shot her a rueful grin and raked his fingers through his hair. 'You also have an annoying habit of making me feel nervous.'

'*I* make *you* feel nervous?' But her mind was still wrapped up with what he had said about wanting her in his life for ever. She desperately wanted to rewind so that she could dwell on that a bit longer. Well, a lot longer. What had he meant? Had she misheard or was that his way of proposing to her in a roundabout manner? Really proposing? Not just asking her to marry him as a pretence…?

Logically, there was no need for him to continue the farce of trying to pull the wool over Alberto's eyes. And Giancarlo was all about logic. Which meant…

Her brain failed to compute.

'I'm nervous now,' Giancarlo said roughly.

'Why?'

'Because there are things I want to say to you. No, things I *need* to say to you. Hell, have I mentioned that that's another annoying trait you have? You make me say things I never thought I would.'

'It's good to be open.'

'I love your homespun pearls of wisdom.' He

held up one hand as though to prevent her from interrupting, although in truth she couldn't have interrupted if she had wanted to, not when that little word *love* had been uttered by him, albeit not exactly in the context she would have liked.

'I never knew how much I had been affected by my past until you came along,' he said in such a low voice that she had to lean forward in the darkness to follow him.

'Sure, I remembered my childhood, but it had been coloured by my mother and after a while her bitterness just became my reality. I accepted it. The financial insecurity was all my father's fault and my job was to know exactly where the blame lay and to make sure that I began rectifying the situation as soon as I was capable of doing that. I never questioned the rights or wrongs of being driven to climb to the top. It felt like my destiny, and anyway I enjoyed it. I was good at it. Making money came naturally to me and if I recognised my mother's inability to control her expenditures then I ignored it. The fact is, in the process, I forgot what it meant to just take each day at a time and learn to enjoy the little things that had nothing to do with making money.

'Am I boring you?' He smiled crookedly at her and Caroline's heart constricted.

'You could never do that,' she breathed huskily, not wanting to disturb the strange, thrilling atmosphere between them.

Giancarlo, who had never suffered a moment's hesitation in his life before, took comfort from that assertion.

'Ditto.' He badly wanted to reach out and touch her. It was an all-consuming craving that he had to fight to keep at bay.

'But you never got involved with anyone. Never had the urge to settle down?' It was a question she desperately needed answering. Yes, he might have been driven to make money—it might have been an ambition that had been planted in him from a young age, when he had been too young to question it and then too old to debate its value—but that didn't mean that he couldn't have formed a lasting relationship somewhere along the way.

'My mother,' Giancarlo said wryly. 'Volatile, embittered, seduced by men who made empty promises and then vanished without a backward glance. I don't suppose she was the ideal role-model. Don't get me wrong, I accepted her and I loved her, but it never occurred to me that I would want someone like that in my life as a partner. I worked all the hours God made, and in a highly stressed environment the last thing I needed was a woman who was high maintenance and I was quietly certain that all women were. Until I met you.'

'I'm not sure that I should take that as a compliment.' But she was beaming. She could barely think straight and her heart was beating like a sledgehammer inside her. Take it as a compliment? She was on a high! She felt as though she had received the greatest compliment of her life! She had felt so inadequate thinking about the exciting, glamorous women he had dated. How could she ever hope to measure up? And yet here he was, reaching deep to find the true essence of her, and filling her with a heady sense of self-confidence that was frankly amazing.

'You're fishing.'

'Okay, you're right. I am. But can you blame me? I've spent weeks trying not to tell you how crazy I am about you.'

Giancarlo grinned and at last reached out and linked his fingers through hers. Warmth spread through him like treacle, heating every part of his body. He rubbed his thumb over hers.

'You're crazy about me,' he murmured with lazy satisfaction and Caroline blushed madly. Liberated from having to hold back what she would otherwise have confessed because she was so open by nature, she felt as though she was walking on cloud nine.

'Madly,' she admitted on a sigh, and when he pulled her towards him she relaxed against his hard body with a sensation of bliss and utter completion. 'I thought you were the most arrogant person on the face of the earth, to start with, but then I don't know what happened. You made me laugh and I began to see a side to you that was so wonderfully complex and fascinating.'

'Complex and fascinating. I like it. Carry on.'

She twisted to look up at him and smiled when he kissed her, his lips tracing hers gently at first, then with hungry urgency. Her breathing quickened and she moaned as he pushed up her top, quickly followed by her bra. He bent his legs slightly, supporting her so that she could lean back in a graceful arch as he began suckling on her nipples, pulling one then the other into his mouth, greedy to taste her.

She understood sufficient Italian now to know that his hoarse utterances were mind-blowingly erotic, although nothing was as erotic as when, temporarily sated, he looked down seriously at her flushed face to say with such fierce tenderness that her heart flipped over, 'I love you. I don't know when it started. I just knew when I was in Milan that I couldn't stand not being close to you. I missed everything about you.

'Meetings and conferences and lawyers and stockpiling wealth faded into insignificance. I was broken up by the way things had ended between us, and I had to get here as quickly as I could because I was so damned scared that I was on the verge of losing you. Damn it, I wondered whether I'd ever had you in the first place!'

It was unbearably touching to know that this big, strong man, so self-assured and controlled, had been uncertain.

'I love you so much,' she whispered.

'Enough to marry me? Nothing short of that will ever be enough.'

EPILOGUE

CAROLINE looked at the assembled guests with a smile. It wasn't a big wedding. Neither of them had wanted that, although they had had to restrain Alberto from his vigorous efforts to have a full-blown wedding of the century.

'Let's wake up these old bores in their big houses,' he had argued with devilish amusement. 'Give them something to talk about for the next ten years!'

They had chosen to be married in the small church close to where Alberto lived and where Giancarlo had grown up. It felt like home to Caroline, especially over the past two months, when the giddy swirl of having her parents over and planning the wedding had swept her off her feet.

She had never been happier. Giancarlo had proven himself to be a convert to the art of working from home and, along with all the marvellous renovations to the villa, had installed an office in one of the rooms from which he could work at his own chosen pace. Which included a great deal of down time with his bride to be.

Her gaze shifted to the man who was now her husband. Amongst the hundred or so guests— friends, family and neighbours who had delight- edly enjoyed reconnecting with Alberto, who had become something of a recluse over the years—he stood head and shoulders above them all.

Right now, he was smiling, chatting to her par- ents, doubtless charming them even more than they had already been charmed, she thought.

Unconsciously, she placed a hand on her stom- ach, and just at that instant their eyes connected. And this time his smile was all for her, locking her into that secret, loving world she shared with him and him alone.

As everyone began moving towards the formal dining-room, onto which a magnificent marquee had been cleverly attached so that the guests could all be seated comfortably for the five-course meal, he strode across to her, pulling her into the small sitting-room, now empty of guests.

'Have I told you how much I love you?' He

curved his hand behind the nape of her neck and tilted her face to his.

'You have. But you need to remind me how much of this is down to Alberto.'

'The wily old fox.' Giancarlo grinned. 'To think that he knew exactly what he was doing when he decided that we were going to be married. Anyone would be forgiven for thinking, listening to his little speech in the drawing-room, that he had masterminded the whole thing.'

Caroline laughed and thought back affectionately to Alberto's smug declaration that anyone in need of match-making should seek him out.

'I know. Still, how can you do anything but smile when you see how thrilled he is that everything worked out according to his plans, if he's to be believed? I heard him telling Tessa the day before yesterday that there was no way he was going to allow us to go our separate ways because we were pig-headed. He would sooner have summoned the ambulance and threatened to jump in unless we came to our senses.'

'He now has a son and a daughter-in-law and you can bet that I'll be raising my glass to him during my after-dinner speech. He deserves it.

You look spectacular tonight. Have I already mentioned that?'

'Yes, but I've always loved it when you repeat yourself.' Her eyes danced with amusement for he never tired of reminding her of his love.

'Have I also told you that I'm hard for you right now?' As if any proof were needed, he guided her hand to where his erection was pressing painfully against his zip. 'It's awkward having to constantly think of trivia to distract myself from the fact that I've spent the past four hours wanting to rip that dress off you.'

Caroline giggled and glanced down at her ivory dress, which was simple but elegant and had cost a small fortune. She was horrified at the thought of Giancarlo ripping it off her, and amazingly turned on by the image at the same time.

'But I guess I'll have to wait for a few more hours until I have you all to myself.' He curved his hand over her breast, gently massaged it just enough for her to feel that tell-tale moisture dampening between her legs, just enough for her eyelids to flutter drowsily and her pulses to begin their steady race.

He kissed the side of her mouth and then dipped

his tongue inside to explore further until she was gasping, so tempted to pull him towards her, even though she knew that there was no way they could abandon their own reception even for the short-est of time.

But she wanted him to herself just for a few moments longer. Just long enough to tell him her news.

'I can't wait for us to be alone,' he murmured fervently, before she could speak. He relin-quished his hold with evident regret and then primly smoothed the ruffled neckline of her dress. 'Talking and laughing, and making love and mak-ing babies, because in case you didn't know that cunning father of mine has already started mak-ing noises about wanting grandchildren while he still has the energy to play with them. And he's not above pulling any stunt he wants if it means he can get his way.'

'That seems to be a family trait but, now that you mention it…' Caroline couldn't contain her happiness a second longer. She smiled radiantly up at him and reached to stroke his cheek, allow-ing her hand to be captured by his. 'You might find that there's not much need to try on the making babies front.'

'What are you telling me?'

'I'm telling you that I'm a week late with my period, and I just couldn't hold off any longer so I did a pregnancy test this morning—and we're going to have a baby. Are you happy?'

Silly question. She knew that he would be. From the man who had made a habit of walking away from involvement, he had become a devoted partner; he would be a devoted husband and she couldn't think of anyone who would be a more devoted father.

The answer in his eyes confirmed everything she already knew.

'My darling,' he said brokenly. 'I am the happiest man on the face of the earth.' He took both her hands in his and kissed them tenderly. 'And my mission is to make sure that you never forget that.'

* * * * *

Mills & Boon® Large Print
October 2012

A SECRET DISGRACE
Penny Jordan

THE DARK SIDE OF DESIRE
Julia James

THE FORBIDDEN FERRARA
Sarah Morgan

THE TRUTH BEHIND HIS TOUCH
Cathy Williams

PLAIN JANE IN THE SPOTLIGHT
Lucy Gordon

BATTLE FOR THE SOLDIER'S HEART
Cara Colter

THE NAVY SEAL'S BRIDE
Soraya Lane

MY GREEK ISLAND FLING
Nina Harrington

ENEMIES AT THE ALTAR
Melanie Milburne

IN THE ITALIAN'S SIGHTS
Helen Brooks

IN DEFIANCE OF DUTY
Caitlin Crews

Mills & Boon® Large Print
November 2012

THE SECRETS SHE CARRIED
Lynne Graham

TO LOVE, HONOUR AND BETRAY
Jennie Lucas

HEART OF A DESERT WARRIOR
Lucy Monroe

UNNOTICED AND UNTOUCHED
Lynn Raye Harris

ARGENTINIAN IN THE OUTBACK
Margaret Way

THE SHEIKH'S JEWEL
Melissa James

THE REBEL RANCHER
Donna Alward

ALWAYS THE BEST MAN
Fiona Harper

A ROYAL WORLD APART
Maisey Yates

DISTRACTED BY HER VIRTUE
Maggie Cox

THE COUNT'S PRIZE
Christina Hollis